END

IN 13 STORIES

Valerie Lioudis   William Stuart   Jack Appell

Robert W. Easton   Ellen A. Easton

Michael Gillett Veronica Smith   T.D. Ricketts

Kevin J Kennedy   Derek Shupert

L. Douglas Hogan   Stefan Lear   Austin James

First edition

Contents

Introduction

THE END!

The world as we know has come to an end. There is destruction and chaos as far as the eye can see. Are you prepared?

THE END COMES IN MANY FORMS, WHICH ONE SPEAKS TO YOU?

Author Valerie Lioudis has assembled an original anthology of stories from a group of today's hottest writers. Inside there are tales of extinction level events, survival in a broken wasteland, a bar at the end of it all, and so much more. This is a collection of new views on the Earth's demise and humanity's will to survive despite it.

With stories from L. Douglas Hogan, Derek Shupert, Kevin J. Kennedy, Veronica Smith, Stefan Lear, Robert W. Easton, Jack Appell, Austin James, Ellen A. Easton, William Stuart, Michael Gillette, T.D. Ricketts and Valerie Lioudis this wildly diverse and entertaining collection is sure to entertain you with each word.

End of the Line by Valerie Lioudis

I had been in line for over an hour and I was still too far away to see the front door of the local drug store. Randy, the not nearly attractive enough older gentleman in front of me, had tried no less than fifteen different approaches to get into my pants. The end of the world has brought out some interesting suppressed personality traits in the population that may have never made their way to the surface without impending doom lingering over all our heads. Mary, the incredibly impatient soccer mom behind me, had been talking obnoxiously loud to someone on her phone for the last half an hour. I should clarify that. She was on speakerphone.

"They damn well better let me pick up all five of my pills. They can't expect the kids to stand here in one of these ridiculous lines waiting for the damn things."

For the first time since she started her conversation, I completely agreed with her. If she was this horrible, what would her children be like? Monsters. They would be monsters. Randy's hand grazed my shoulder in a not at all welcome way to get my attention. Moments like this had become all that more tricky.

1

A single wrong move could end up with you getting sent to the great beyond faster far quicker than Armageddon.

"What if I told you I would wait out this line for you, and all you had to do was come by tonight to pick up your pill? I could even make you dinner. I still have more than enough supplies to make decent meal."

"I'm good. My boyfriend's family owns a farm." *Lies, all lies.* "And we haven't dealt with any of the shortages. They didn't need to loot either."

"Oh. Might have been nice if you mentioned him earlier. If you didn't notice, I have been trying to ask you out."

Good Lord. "I am so sorry. I can be so dense sometimes. This whole end of the world thing has turned me into a real space cadet. You understand, right?"

"Yeah. Especially a pretty little thing like you who had her whole life in front ahead of her. This whole thing must be devastating." *Groan.* "You know... there is still time to have a few adventures. Try some things you have never tried before."

"I have the next thirty days planned out to the fullest." *More lies.* "My dad always said if the world was ending the powers that be wouldn't let us in on it. They would want us to keep grinding on like the good little cogs that we are right up until the minute it all ends. I guess he was close. Thirty days isn't much time."

Finally, he had a more serious look to his face. "Your dad was right, sweetheart. They never had an intention in telling us plebs. If it hadn't been for those hacked emails getting released, we would have never found out, and we wouldn't be here in line waiting for our free sleeping pills."

Maybe, he can hold it together long enough to have a serious conversation. "My dad said if the reporters weren't so busy playing favorites we might have known a long time ago. I just wonder how they convinced the scientists to keep it quiet for so long. I can't get one or two of my friends to keep a secret without blabbing it to every stinking person we know. They must have threatened them, or something."

"That is probably going to go down as the last big mystery. At this point no one cares anymore, and the next 30 days are sure to be a free for all."

"I hope not!" A shrill voice cut into our conversation. *Well, well, well. Mary has decided to get off her damn phone.* "After this little nightmare, I am going home, loading everyone and heading off to parts unknown."

"Ummm, cupcake?" *God, he is so condescending.* Randy was using that voice that adults use when explaining a difficult subject to a child. "What's your plan for food and gas? You realize that yesterday was the last day anyone will ever go to work, right?"

"That can't be true! There are people handing out the pills today. They can't be the only ones who feel obligated to do their jobs. The government should step in and do something. They could force the people to do their work." Her voice got less sure as she tried to rationalize her train of thought.

Some people could be so stupid.

"They offered these saps a one-way trip to paradise, all for one day of passing out pills. Do yourself a favor and make sure you keep your pills ready if you are going to follow through with that plan. One wrong turn and you guys could end up stranded in the middle of the woods, or worse the city. It is a good idea to have an exit strategy."

Well, that did it. The phone was back out again, and she turned her back to us, which was strange since she insisted

3

in keeping her calls on speaker, so privacy was not the issue. It was most likely symbolic, but neither of us cared enough to be offended.

"Way to burst her dream." My words oozed with sarcasm, but I was grateful that he said something. "It wouldn't be a horrible plan for someone who had some skills, a plan, and a big ass gun."

"I like the way you think. You aren't as naive as you look."

Gee, thanks. "Momma didn't raise no fool." I patted my hip where I would have kept my gun if I had one on me. *Lies, upon lies, upon lies.* "What are you going to do for the next thirty?"

The line suddenly moved forward a hundred or so feet, and for a second I felt like we were making progress. It stopped as quickly as it began, and we were back feeling like we were in bumper to bumper traffic, minus the comfy seat to ride it out in.

"Damn, I thought we would get closer to the door. Oh, well. I guess I get to enjoy the scenery a bit longer." His eyes crawled up and down my body. *Groan, I wish I had worn a shirt with a higher neckline.* "Hmmm. The next thirty? I plan on sitting back nice and safe in my home with all the supplies and protection I could ever need." This part wasn't much louder than a whisper, and he kept nervously checking around to see if anyone was listening. "I'm gonna sit back and enjoy the show. You?"

Before I could answer, Mary was shoved into my back almost knocking me to the ground.

"I said shut your stupid freakin mouth bitch!" The woman who had been trapped behind Mary screamed as her veins pulsated on her forehead. "I am sick to shit of you making your god damned phone calls public!" *I could not agree more.*

"You didn't have to push me!" Mary's whine was like nails

4

on a chalkboard. "You could have just asked me."

"Jesus, if she can't handle a line in suburbia, how is she going to make it out on the open road? You can just tell that she is the one that wears the pants in her family. Her husband must be a real piece of work."

I reached down to help pull Mary up, but she smacked my hand away determined to regain some of her dignity. *Randy's right. If she can't tell someone who wants to hurt her from someone who wants to help her, she is screwed.* "We're going to be in this line a lot longer than any of us want to admit. You might want to figure out a way to stop pissing everyone off and start making friends. I'm going to say this once, because I think no one has told you yet, but there isn't anyone to protect you anymore. If you push someone too far, it may not work out for you."

She drug her sweatshirt sleeve across her face wiping away the snotty mess left behind from getting knocked upside the head. "I wish you would all just leave me alone. You're wrong. You are all wrong. The last thirty days are going to be beautiful. People are inherently good, and they will do the right thing."

"Then why are you in line?" Randy taunted. "If you are so sure of the love-fest that is about to happen, you shouldn't need a suicide pill."

"Screw you." She hissed.

"You couldn't get so lucky, but maybe after I've had all the tens, I could slum it with a four."

Damn. Randy is savage.

"You are disgusting. I would never sleep with a man like you, and don't think we haven't all noticed you trying to crawl all over this child." Her face went all smug, like she had delivered the death blow.

"Damn straight, I have been trying to crawl all over her. One,

5

she isn't a child. That shit is gross. And two, your problem is that you still don't seem to get it. We have thirty days left. Thirty days to do just about anything that will make us happy and not freak out that on day thirty-one people won't exist anymore. So, I hope to spend my last month on Earth screwing anyone that catches my eye, eating as much trans-fat as I can find, and blowing shit up. If I am lucky, I might even manage to get wasted a few more times. Then, on day twenty nine, I am going to say my prayers, down a bottle of jack, and take one of these pills we are waiting around for, so I won't have to feel the impact of the space rock that is coming to wipe us all out."

"Here, here!" Cheered a man a few people back.

"What a waste. Sounds like you wasted your life, and you are going to waste what is left of it. I feel bad for you. I get to spend my last thirty days with people I love, and you have nothing. Not one thing of value in that little list you gave. So, maybe you don't get it. We only have thirty days left and there isn't enough time for you to finally find something of value. That makes you jealous and pathetic."

Oh, damn. Maybe, she is right. I don't really have anyone. I will never get married. I am never going to have kids. What did my life mean, if anything?

While I was stuck in my head questioning my entire existence, Randy took action. And that action was punching Mary square in the jaw.

"That's going to hurt for the next thirty days. Maybe it will stop you from running your mouth about shit you don't know." He said and then spit on her unconscious body.

Everyone in line stood still for a few minutes, unable to react to what just happened in front of them.

Is this the new normal? Men can just hit women now, and no one

6

cares?

We were all awoken from our trance as the line began to move again. This time we were going to get in the front door. I looked back to see people stepping over Mary's body. No one was willing to lose their spot in line helping her, myself included. The door was so close. This nightmare might be over soon. I stepped over the threshold and the fluorescent lights poured down onto my skin. What used to be a very mundane, and slightly annoying occurrence, had me feeling nostalgic. This may be the last time that I ever step foot in a sterile and cold retail place. That was something I never thought I would miss.

The door clicked shut three people after me, and with it all the troubles of the outside world disappeared behind it. Inside the line was moving constantly. Where outside, we were stuck together long enough to engage in small talk, indoors the movement kept us from needing the distraction of each other. Randy had mysteriously forgotten that I even existed, which was fine by me.

We wove in and out of the aisles, which were picked bare from the looting that occurred a few days ago. I was reminded of a going out of business sale on the last day where only the unsellable garbage and fixtures were left. The whole world was one giant going out of business sale now. As I shuffled my feet my mind drifted off to the stores that most likely stood stocked still. Cases of jewelry, high end couture, and purses as far as the eye could see, but I bet the most coveted things two weeks ago were useless garbage now.

Before I knew it, the a kind looking woman in her sixties was calling me up to the counter.

"Do you have your slip, dear?"

"Absolutely. Here you go." I handed her the crumpled piece

THE END IN 13 STORIES

of paper. I tend to fidget, so the paper took a beating waiting in line outside. "Thank you for doing this."

"Aww, sweetheart, I would say it was the right thing to do, but I'm here for the free trip."

"Good for you. I would have jumped all over that offer."

"Oh, I am sure you have someone waiting to spend the last few days with, but not me. My husband died a few years ago, and the kids are across the country with their families. It was an easy choice for me. Looks like everything is all set here. I scanned your paper. Is it ok if I toss it?"

"Why would anyone want to keep it?"

"Who knows. Some people are just collectors. I got yelled at when I threw a few away earlier today, so I just ask now. Makes my day easier."

"People are weird."

"You ain't kidding. Now, remember, when you take it, you will be asleep in less than five minutes. It will be all over in ten. Painless." She said as she handed the small envelope to me. "Have a great month!" she waved me away with actual sincerity.

We were herded out the back door. I half expected Randy to be waiting for me outside but was pleasantly surprised when he wasn't. My truck was far too large for someone of my size, but I loved her none the less. Clicking the radio on I was greeted by static from most of the stations that were preprogrammed into my radio. Using scan, I was able to get three stations to come in. The Christian one had a man preaching from the Book of Revelations. *No thank you. It is far too late for that.*

Choice number two was a college station that had been hijacked by one of the DJs who was playing clips of his favorite songs and then ranting about their value to society. This would have been almost entertaining except he was into screamo, and there was no way I could handle that even in clips. Last, but not least, was the local radio personality who usually complained about the current affairs of our state, who had finally found a way to not be obnoxious for the final month. He was letting listeners call in to tell their favorite memory from life and request a song.

As I pulled up to the house, I checked my pocket to make sure my precious cargo was still sitting where I shoved it. The front of the house looked the same as when I left so many hours ago. After watching Mary take one to the head, I figured I should be a bit more cautious, at least for now. I clicked the door open, which was the universal signal for Machiavelli, my cat, to come running to greet me. His soft fur tickled each of my ankles as he did his signature take down move, the figure eight.

"Let's get you some food. I am sure you are hungry." I said as I scratched his chin.

Nothing says love like a fresh can of tuna. The good stuff, too, none of the cheap garbage for my baby. I pulled the prize out of my pocket and unwrapped the paper. Hiding pills from animals is a work of art. You must make sure that every part is hidden, or the cat will just spit it back out.

"Here you are sweetie-pie. Mommy loves you so much."

I lay across the tile floor and pet Machiavelli while he scarfed down his favorite treat. *No need for you to suffer.* Before the bowl was even empty, the effects set in. He curled up tight against my chest, and I stroked his body until I felt him go still. As I stood, I lay a small kiss on his head. *Sleep tight, my sweet prince. Soon enough, we will meet again.*

I straightened my shirt and pulled myself together. No time for tears. There was barely enough time for the plans that I had

THE END IN 13 STORIES

made. The Art of War sat in contrast to the other books sitting on my bookshelf. It clicked open the false wall as I pulled on it, and I was able to access my favorite room in my home. A ten by ten armory hidden from the whole world. Rows of weapons, meticulously cared for and displayed, awaited me. The hardest thing would be choosing which ones to take.

"I hope thirty days is enough. Last man standing wins."

End of the Line by Carl Bolton @guerrillaillustrator on Instagram

Author Bio

While she mostly focuses on Horror, Valerie Lioudis is a multi-genre author who has been known to dabble in post apocalyptic, science fiction, and even metaphysical stories. The common thread with Valerie's work is her constant sarcasm, and love for bringing the unexpected to her readers. She loves the art of writing a short story, and has merged that with giving back to those in need. Many of the anthologies she is involved with donate their proceeds to groups near and dear to her. Two of the causes she is proud to say she has helped raise money for through writing are Veterans and Breast Cancer charities. She is an active member of the Reanimated Writers Facebook group, and can found there to answer any questions you may have about any of her work. Come join the horde, we would love to have you.

amazon.com/author/valerielioudis
instagram.com/valerielioudis/
facebook.com/AuthorValerieLioudis/
aftershockzombieseries.com

Still Here Somehow by William Stuart

As we used to say, God moves in mysterious ways. At least he did. I've no idea how he moves anymore. I don't know if he even exists anymore. I don't know much of anything since it all came down. All I know is that there is nothing left except endless fields of burnt rock. I suppose there is still something that could be classified as an atmosphere, if you were playing real loose with the definition. And me. I'm still here. Somehow.

Truth be told, I'm not sure what the final straw was. Everything seemed pretty normal, in that there was terror and atrocity all over just as there had always been. Whatever it was that we called the news stoked the fires of discontent around the clock so they could sell one more prescription drug, one more fast food value meal; which of course didn't help people think clearly. Governments were constantly rattling their sabers and pushing their pieces across the board. I was one of those pieces getting moved across the board.

If you're thinking I was some sort of Special Forces badass that somehow fought my way through the apocalypse, you'd be wrong. I was no soldier, and never had any intention of becoming one. I worked in supply chain logistics; just a regular guy doing a regular job until things got so bad that the government brought back the draft. Then I was just a regular guy getting moved around and yelled at by commanders who resented the draftees for having not volunteered years ago.

Still, conscription was nothing new. In fact, the two or three decades in which it wasn't policy were the anomalies. Wars and interventions were commonplace through all of human history and looking back, although it ended the way it did, it probably would have worked itself out and in time. It would have been remembered by history as a period of great suffering, but not as bad as World War One or Two. Things had not only been bad before, they had been far worse. Except for a few Doomsday preppers and certain religious groups, who always predict these sorts of things, nobody expected what would happen next was the Biblical Apocalypse.

I'd never been much for religion. If anything, I was some sort of non-practicing protestant. Went to church a few times as a kid, then mostly weddings and funerals as an adult. My views on issues such as faith and sin and whatever were vague at best. I suppose you could say I was... apatheistic? But I learned enough about end-time prophecy from movies and books that when events began to unfold, it was pretty clear what was going on, even to a heathen like me.

So much is clearer now, of course. The world finally got tired of the Middle East and the United Nations formed a coalition to essentially conquer and occupy several sovereign nations. Everyone was just so tired of terrorism and jihad that very few protested. Some street preachers pointed out that this was how Armageddon happened. But most people, myself included, just wanted to close it down: get some law and order established

14

and stop having an entire region of the world used as a breeding ground for suicidal fanatics. So, they sent in the troops.

Of course, nothing much happened at first. The major powers, after sending their armies, wanted to ensure that they all got their proper pieces of the pie before they threw in, and in spectacular fashion, they failed to agree on anything. Armies afield, standing shoulder to shoulder, waiting for orders... We didn't know if the man or woman standing next to us was friendly or hostile from one day to the next. We just hung out there, in the desert, waiting for something to happen. Then one day the sky became very dark, as if a major storm was about to hit. The ground shook and thunder rolled and then pebbles began falling from the sky. At first we thought it was hail, which would have been unusual enough, but it was raining rocks. We assumed that maybe a conflict started and the stone shower was the result of an explosion somewhere out of sight. What happened next was that a whole lot of people around the world simply vanished. A whole lot of people. Well, a lot fewer than you might expect given what had happened just then, but it was still a lot.

But we didn't have time to contemplate any of that, and I don't know what I might have thought about it if I did. After the shower of rocks, it was quiet. The thunder from before had faded and we were just hanging out there in our tent cities waiting for the next move. Someone happened to look up and though it was early in the afternoon, the moon and stars were visible in the darkened sky and everything was a crimson red color. It was deathly silent. For miles, as far as you could see, the armies of the great powers of Earth stood staring at the moon, mouths agape, in the eerie noontime darkness.

It took about half an hour for the effect to wear off. Commanders started shouting orders at grunts and we were told to stop jerking off and get back to our posts. I had happened to be off duty at the moment, but got pulled aside by a sergeant who put me on guard duty because he couldn't find the man who was supposed to be there. Of course, that man and many others went AWOL that day, never to be seen again, but nobody ever looked for them too hard.

As I was heading to my station, a siren sounded and frantic orders to evacuate came through in several languages. Barely controlled chaos ensued as coalition forces from all over the world attempted to move themselves and their equipment to higher ground. You see, our central base of operations was in a huge open space that would soon be a shallow lake the size of Rhode Island. Whatever had caused the stone rain earlier had triggered a massive tsunami, rather, several massive tsunamis around the world, one of which was heading straight for us. We were far enough inland not to be in too much danger of drowning, but tents, gear, generators, and vehicles were all in jeopardy. We scrambled for higher ground, getting nowhere near enough stuff out of the way before the water rose. But then, the water stopped rising, opting instead to mix with the sand and sink the remaining vehicles, and at least a few thousand people, in an ocean of quicksand.

The world was shocked. All over the globe, cities fell to tidal waves that went sometimes as far as two hundred miles inland. Millions perished in the floods and countless numbers died in the days that followed. Relief workers were rallied, but the destruction was overwhelming. The coalition of forces were immediately sent home to help with relief and recovery efforts. More people would have probably been aware of the rapture and its implications, but there was never time. After that, things got quite confusing.

Chaos ruled. Even in the deeply landlocked areas unaffected by the floods there were shortages and fighting, crime and unrest was everywhere. Several seats of government had been swallowed by the sea, with some nations' entire leadership swept away and others greatly diminished. Central authority broke down globally as the strain on the systems became too much. Those of us who had made it through so far unscathed wondered if we would ever see anything resembling normal again. Then he came.

So much clarity in retrospect.

Joshua Black. Young, good-looking, well spoken. He'd been a freshman senator prior to the disaster. At some point he took control and began calling shots. Again, I think people would have been more vigilant if they hadn't just been through, and were still living in, one of the largest natural disasters in history. But vigilant or not, it wouldn't have mattered. Joshua Black was brilliant. Within a day or two of his taking charge the government started working again. Those who were left after the storm suddenly and quietly went back to work. He mobilized relief efforts. He reorganized the armed and police forces. He was charismatic and funny and the nation and the world had a new favorite son.

Almost all military personnel had been withdrawn from bases around the world to assist in domestic relief efforts. Entire cities up and down both coasts had been wiped off the map. I was stationed at a refugee center near Dallas when Black announced his candidacy for President. I was at another refugee center on the outskirts of what used to be Los Angeles two years later when he declared martial law and announced mandatory chip identification for all residents after a terrorist attack and an

17

assassination attempt. I was no idiot and given the sequence of events, there were plenty of clapboards hailing Black as the Antichrist. Of course he was. Everybody with half a brain at least suspected it. But when he made pacts with the heads of various religions, including the Pope, all suspicion ceased. Or at least nobody talked about it in public for fear of what might happen if he found out about it.

There were protests all over the world about having to be chipped but they were really half-hearted. People were hungry and tired and traumatized. There were still places in the world where those who drowned in the tidal waves hadn't yet been gathered or buried. Areas that had once been fertile fields were now brackish swamps where nothing grew and where corpses floated. Food was in short supply. I had been working nearly fourteen hours a day for at least four years and the lines at our stations had never gotten shorter. People were sick, they were tired, and they basically did whatever they needed to do to get through another day. A microchip got them a measure of barley or corn or whatever we had in our trucks that day. Or rather, it gave them a better chance. We rarely had enough food to give to everyone in the line. A chip got you about a 50/50 shot though. Which was better than nothing.

I spent most of my time being shuffled around from one relief duty to another. I had long since given up on getting out of the military. We were in constant shortage and every time I had a review, my time was extended by six months or two years. At this point I was nearing fifty years old and had been on active duty for a little less than ten years. All over the world, economies were crashing. Power was being consolidated among the few remaining large powers. The Middle East was still famous for its terror and strife, and Joshua Black, at some point, decided to revisit the old plan of putting an end to it once and for all. Unfortunately, this time there was no coalition. This time it was the U.S., China, and Russia squaring off in the desert trying to take control and keep control before any of the others could act. I was on the other side of the world, too old to participate in combat, but in a guard post somewhere near Denver when Armageddon began.

It was a no-holds-barred fight. All the major players hit one another with everything they had and everything they had worked well. The devastation was complete. Several cities across the globe were bombed, either conventional or nuclear nobody knew for sure. By the end of it all most everything and everyone on that side of the world was ash. And we got the fallout on our side too. The sky got dark. Things got very, very cold. Winds howled day and night. Everyone knew it was the end of the world. By now, nobody, even the most passionate non-believer, could deny what had just occurred. But there was nothing to do for it but keep on moving.

Those few of us who were left became fewer. Some wandered off into the dark, others just gave up and did other things. I didn't know what to think. I'd always been a pretty ambivalent about my job and duty. It was less about anything other than I had been ordered to be where I was and so I just went. There were no orders anymore. Just lots of wailing and occasional bright flashes followed by somber rumbling far off in the distance. There were monstrous things screaming out there, in the dark. Screaming and dying, and falling so hard they shook the ground. When the noises got too close, I finally ran away.

The war between the angels and the demons lasted for a long time. I can never be sure how long because it was a perpetual thing that happened just outside of my vision, but it was years, perhaps decades before the final scream was silenced. In the meantime I had found a cave and hidden there. Some unlucky traveler had provisioned this place before I'd arrived but he never came back. Nobody would ever come back. I didn't know it at the time, but in the midst of the final battle between the powers of Heaven and Hell, I'd become the lone human survivor. As the screams and the roars and the horror played itself out, I huddled in my little cave.

The battle raged on as I began to move through my provisions. At first I'd gathered that the cave was stocked with enough food, water, and fuel for a family of four to survive for a year. I began marking the days on the wall of the cave. A year passed and my foodstuffs held strong. Two years and I was still okay. Five years and I finally finished the last can of hickory smoked tuna fish. I had scratched a line into the wall every time I saw light coming through the front of my cave. I couldn't be sure, sometimes the days came more often than it seemed they should. Other times, the light didn't come for months. The battle outside continued, but it was ebbing. Slowing down in both frequency and intensity of events.

At some point it occurred to me that it had to have been at least a week or two since I had eaten. It didn't hurt; I was not weak or uncomfortable. It was merely a realization. It had also been a long time since I'd heard any of the monsters outside. I decided it was time to chance a look.

I couldn't have possibly been prepared for what I saw.

Everything had been torn asunder. As far as the eye could see were barren fields of burnt rock, except the eye could not see very far for the thick smog that hung onto the lifeless husk that used to be a planet. There was no wind to move the smoke. Nothing was left. The whole place was simply gone.

I set out to find others. Certainly someone else had found some similar cover that had kept them safe from the demons as they raged. But no, there was no one. Not a single soul. I began to walk and to call. I walked until my legs could no longer carry me and my lungs burned from crying out to someone, anyone, "HELLO! IS THERE ANYBODY OUT THERE? CAN ANYONE HEAR ME?"

Occasionally I was answered by a mocking echo of my own voice, but never that of another. I finally stopped calling out. I wandered for weeks, for months, and finally, for years. I've traversed canyons that used to be seas. I've been to highest and lowest points. I've never found food, water, another person, or even two stones stacked one upon the other. There's nothing. Just this endless smoke in this endless twilight in this endless expanse of burnt rock. I've considered going to the top of a mountain and jumping off but I intuitively know that I won't die. No, I'd maybe just get hurt really badly for my troubles. I don't know why I'm here. I don't know why, out of all the billions of people on the planet; people who were much better than me and much, much worse, that it should be me that got left behind. God just closed up shop on Earth and threw away the key and left me here to kick rocks.

But, as they used to say, God moves in mysterious ways. At least he did. I've no idea how he moves anymore. I don't know if he even exists anymore. I don't know much of anything since it all came down. All I know is that there is nothing left except endless fields of burnt rock. I suppose there is still something that could be classified as an atmosphere, if you were playing real loose with the definition. And me. I'm still here. Somehow.

Author Bio

William Stuart lives in Texas with his wife, two daughters, and a grumpy old dog. When he's not writing scary stories, you can find him taking on way too many projects and hobbies at a time, reading comics, magazines, or books about monsters, or sweating in the garage trying to figure out how to bring dead things to life.

Find his work on Amazon at https://www.amazon.com/William-Stuart/e/B07HHK2X5F/

Underground by Jack Appell

"Breathe in..."

His breathing had subconsciously fallen into rhythm with the ticking away of seconds on his wristwatch.

"Breathe out... breathe in..."

Tick, tick, tick.

"Breathe out..."

He remained seated for a moment as a feeling of calm radiated through him. Meditation was vital in times such as these. Preservation of mind was as important as preservation of body and supplies. Sometimes he wished he had discovered it before the events that forced him to retreat into his bunker. He noticed that he was generally less angry and more capable of focusing after meditating.

Wyatt slowly extended his limbs as he opened his eyes, stretching the stiffness away as he stood. He reached above him until his fingertips brushed the cold ceiling. Wyatt was six feet tall, just about the maximum height to be able to comfortably stand and stretch in the small rooms that the bunker provided. He brushed his shaggy brown hair out of his eyes and looked around the room.

"Sugar?"

He quickly made the bed and sat down on it. He looked towards the bedroom door as he reached for his shoes, absent-mindedly wondering where she could have gone as he finished putting his socks and shoes on. It was a small bunker compared to some luxury models so she couldn't have gone far, but it wasn't like her to not respond. Wyatt stood and grabbed his belt off the nightstand.

"Sugar!" He called out again as he threaded the belt through the loops, stopping about three quarters of the way to slip a fixed blade knife in sheath between the belt loops on his right hip. "Where are you?" He listened for some kind of response as he finished with his belt. Silence. Panic began to swell as Wyatt left the bedroom and turned into the kitchen.

The bunker consisted of two main compartments, each one measuring 65 feet in length and 15 feet in width, laid side by side with a six-foot-wide alley between them for wires, ventilation, and such. These compartments were connected at one end by a mudroom, through which the generator and stairwell to the outside were also accessible. At the opposite end, each section had its own escape tunnel.

One compartment accommodated the entire living space. It closely resembled a single wide mobile home in design. The main entrance was situated off the mudroom and led into a hallway, with the bathroom on the right next to the door. The hallway continued through a sort of breezeway which was designed to hold bunks, however, Wyatt had installed a storage closet on the left and a communication center with a ham radio, AM/FM receiver, and video surveillance of the bunker's entry points on the right. Beyond the breezeway was

24

a dining area/living room/office with a computer desk next to the command center, a table beside the storage closet, couch, television, DVD player, and shelves full of movies and books. Just beyond the living room was the kitchen and then a doorway to the bedroom. When Wyatt stood just outside the bedroom door, he could see most of the bunker, apart from the front door, the interior of the bathroom, and the nooks and crannies.

Wyatt moved through the living room quickly, glancing under the table and computer desk as he approached the breezeway. Just as he was passing the bunk platform that served as a command center, something caught his eye. He switched on the light and dropped to his hands and knees.

"Sugar! What are you doing under there? You scared me half to death!"

Sugar lifted her head to look at Wyatt before stretching and yawning, then slowly crawled out of her hiding space. Wyatt sat back on the floor with his back against the storage closet for a moment, letting the panic wash away. Sugar walked over to him and licked the side of his face.

"Well, good morning to you, too. You scared the hell out of me. What are you doing sleeping out here anyway?" Wyatt scratched behind her ears as he questioned her. Sugar just smiled and wagged her tail in response. "Well," he continued, "I guess you probably want to eat some breakfast, huh?"

Wyatt rose to his feet and turned back toward the kitchen as Sugar led the way. They had been together for four years, since he had bought her through an online ad for $25. She was a mutt, part boxer, part pit-bull, which meant that she wasn't quite as big in size or as short in the snout as a full boxer. She was mostly fawn, with a dark chocolate face and matching strip down the center of her back. The family that owned her mother, Sugar

25

Bear, had opted not to dock the tails or ears on the puppies and Wyatt couldn't imagine putting a puppy through unnecessary pain, so she was blessed with floppy ears and a curly tail to chase.

Before retreating to the bunker, as things began to decline and it became clear that going underground would eventually be necessary, Wyatt had spent a good deal of time preparing the bunker and stockpiling supplies. The bunker was a pre-existing structure when he had bought the house and land above it. It was one of the main selling points and the reason the seller could get away with such a high asking price. When he placed the ad, he had included little Easter eggs which would indicate to a knowledgeable prepper that the property included such a feature, resulting in the high price tag. This stroke of extremely good luck meant that Wyatt could spend more of his budget furnishing, reinforcing, and stocking the shelter since the cost of the bunker itself was included in his monthly mortgage payments.

Wyatt bought Sugar Ray the same week that he moved into the house. He had never lived on his own before and had been looking forward to the peace of not having a roommate or significant other to deal with, but he quickly discovered that peace and solitude often bring their friend loneliness with them. Unwilling to share his new home with another person just yet, he opted to get a dog instead. It turned out to be one of the best decisions he had ever made. Sugar was everything Wyatt wanted in a friend, a hiking and camping partner, someone to go for long rides in the jeep with, and none of the small talk or social pressure. She quickly became his best friend, and from the very beginning, wherever Wyatt went, she went as well.

Most of Wyatt's prepper friends warned him that bringing

a dog into the bunker would create a new set of problems to be dealt with such as extra medical supplies, storing food, and creating space for her to run and relieve herself, but as Wyatt saw it, he didn't have a wife or kids to stock supplies for so he had space to spare. He kept Sugar on a diet that consisted of dry kibble and a variety of homemade meals and treats which were made from ingredients he would already have in the bunker stores anyway. He also fitted the door to each compartment with a doggy door so that she could go between the "house" and the "yard" unassisted. Then, he divided the second unit into three parts. The mudroom entry led directly into a gym that had been outfitted with equipment for Wyatt and a few pieces of equipment that he had modified to keep Sugar in shape, such as a treadmill and a weight sled with a dog harness attached to the cable. Beyond the gym was a plant nursery, followed by an "open air" garden and dog run, which was basically just a room that he painted to look like a backyard with picket fence painted onto the lower portion of the walls, some trees and flowers, and a blue sky painted onto the ceiling and upper parts of the walls. He had decided to splurge and install realistic looking Astroturf on the floor, mostly for Sugar's enjoyment, but also in the hopes that it would help alleviate the feeling of cabin fever that he anticipated. Cleaning up after Sugar required little more than a pooper scooper, a little bit of water, and some disinfectant. He also upgraded the ceiling light fixture to accommodate heat bulbs to simulate the feeling of being outside as much as possible, though he more often used regular bulbs to conserve energy and preserve safety. On a whim, he had purchased two oscillating floor fans, which he painted to look like giant pinwheels. When he was feeling nostalgic for the surface, he would put a heat bulb in, turn on the fans, and lay on the floor on a towel with his eyes closed, pretending he was lying on a hillside enjoying a sunny, breezy day.

Sugar stretched as Wyatt measured rolled oats and poured them into a saucepan of boiling water, giving them a quick stir. He reached across the counter and pulled the cinnamon off the spice rack and grabbed the sugar jar. Sugar sat and watched as he moved to the end of the counter and opened the lid on the airtight container that kept her kibble safe. He quickly measured and poured some into her bowl as the oats boiled away. Wyatt snapped the container closed, placed the bowl on the counter, and turned off the heat under the oatmeal. He mixed in some sugar and gave it a quick stir, then scooped about a quarter cup into Sugar's bowl before adding cinnamon to the rest.

As the oatmeal cooled, Wyatt went about his morning routine. Even though he hadn't had any luck contacting anyone on the outside in the three months they had been in the bunker, every morning, Wyatt followed a routine of communications efforts as though it had been prescribed by a doctor. First, he powered on the communications array. Wyatt didn't know much about telecommunications, so he had hired a friend of a friend to install the set up. The young man had come highly recommended and, upon finishing, had guaranteed Wyatt that, if there was internet to be found after the apocalypse, Wyatt would pick it up. He powered on his cell phone and placed it beside the AM/FM radio, which he also switched on.

As his cellphone cycled through its startup process, he scanned through the radio from the lowest frequency to the highest on FM and back down again, then, upon finding nothing but static, switched to AM and repeated the process. Hearing nothing more than the same looped emergency broadcast messages, Wyatt switched the radio off again. He picked up his cellphone and checked for a signal from the network. As the phone searched for a signal, he opened the image gallery and scrolled through thumbnails of old memories and loved ones that he hadn't been able to reach in months.

As the last few lights on the array began to blink, Wyatt put the phone down and reached under the desk to power the computer on. He watched the screen just long enough to make sure that it started its normal boot up process, then picked the cellphone back up and continued scrolling through thumbnails. After a minute, he closed the gallery and opened his voicemails. His phone had come with a feature that allowed him to save his voicemails to his phone and listen to them without a being connected to a network. He had saved messages from most of his family members so that he could hear their voices whenever he wanted. He scrolled through the messages for a moment, but decided that he might be a little bit too nostalgic at the moment to start listening to voices of misplaced loved ones. Instead, he shut the phone off and turned his attention to the ham radio. Being the primary source of communication, the ham radio was connected to a backup generator along with the surveillance system to ensure that both remained operable at all times. Wyatt made sure everything was working and set up properly, then adjusted the volume until he heard a voice.

Wyatt had listened to the recorded message numerous times a day since going underground, scrutinizing it for any indication that a new message might be playing in its place. Upon reaching the end of the loop, each time, Wyatt would find himself unable to hide from his disappointment. It was, without fail, the exact same message every time.

"This is an emergency broadcast from the Gaston County

Sheriff's Department. We urge all survivors who are in need of medical care or emergency evacuation to proceed immediately to one of the following locations: Gaston County Sheriff's Department headquarters in Gastonia, Ashbrook High School in Gastonia, Stuart Cramer High School in Cramerton, South Point High School in Belmont, or Mount Holly Middle School in Mount Holly. Emergency personnel will be available at each location. Please be advised that each person will be permitted one small bag for all personal effects, including clothing, medication, etc. Food will be available at evacuation points for as long as supplies last."

Pause. Repeat.

That was the entire message. It almost made Wyatt laugh. The world had gone to shit and all that local law enforcement could do for the people it was responsible for was repeat a 30 second message that offered little help and even less hope. He switched the ham to a frequency that he and his family had chosen for finding each other should there ever be an emergency in which they couldn't otherwise communicate and lowered the volume a bit before turning his attention to the computer monitor. He opened the network settings in an effort to connect to the internet, quickly gave up and shut the computer back down before switching off the entire array.

Sugar sat up as Wyatt leaned back in his chair and stretched. He turned his attention to a monitor that was anchored to the wall above the communications set up, on which four security camera feeds ran simultaneously, each taking up a quarter of the screen. There were wide-angle day/night security cameras trained on the exit points for each of the emergency tunnels, one aimed at the surface door at the top of the mudroom stairwell, and one that was positioned approximately halfway up the driveway that provided a view of the front yard, which Wyatt felt would be the most likely point of approach for any unwelcome visitors. That monitor and the cameras, along with the ham radio, were wired into both the main generator and a separate, constant power supply that was backed up by a small generator powered by solar panels so that Wyatt would never have to wait to see the exits in the event of an emergency. Both were connected to single-board computer which was no bigger than a cellphone which was tasked with supporting those two applications and nothing more.

"Nothing, Suge. Nothing," Wyatt stated flatly as he began to rise. "Sometimes, I don't know if that's a blessing or a curse."

Wyatt headed back to the kitchen, picked up Sugar's bowl and placed it on the floor beside his seat at the table. He picked up the saucepan that he had made the oatmeal in and brought it to the table with him, stopping to grab a spoon from the dish rack along the way. As he sat down and took a bite, he looked down and saw that Sugar was watching him intently.

"Don't judge me. It saves water," he said through a mouthful of oatmeal. "You should eat," he continued. "It's leg day. We have to stay in shape. You're going to need the energy." Sugar stared in response. "Oh!" Wyatt exclaimed. "How could I forget?"

Wyatt jogged back to the kitchen, grabbed the cinnamon off the counter, and returned to his seat. He sprinkled a tiny shake over Sugar's bowl and placed it on the table as Sugar finally turned her attention towards her breakfast. "Diva," he laughed as they both started eating.

After spending the better part of an hour in the gym, Wyatt checked on his plants in the nursery while Sugar continued through to the yard area. Although he mostly grew herbs to season the bland bunker food, he was also working on growing some fresh vegetables through a domestic hydroponic gardening set-up. Unfortunately, gardening wasn't something that he was highly skilled at and he found that it wasn't a talent you could hope to develop quickly out of necessity. It required knowledge, patience, and plenty of practice, and while Wyatt had several books on gardening in general, hydroponic gardening specifically, and other "For Dummies" and beginner's books to reference, as well as an abundance of patience to commit, what he lacked was the practice. As a result, Wyatt ended up spending a fair amount of time in the nursery each day checking on his plants and reading in search of answers to the many questions he had.

After researching different theories on how to perk up wilted lettuce, grow a fruit bearing tree indoors hydroponically, and a few other things, Wyatt made his way to the yard. It was close to lunch time and his stomach was beginning to growl. He glanced around the room but Sugar had long since made her way back over to the living area. He turned around and headed toward the mudroom door, looking around each room as he passed through, making sure Sugar hadn't decided to take a nap in a new hiding spot.

As he passed through the door into the mudroom, he made a quick left into the generator room. He clicked on the overhead light and slowly walked around the massive thing, pausing at the rear to inspect the exhaust fan and the pipe that funneled the fumes to the surface. Satisfied that everything was working properly, Wyatt turned the light off and left the room, closing the door behind him as he turned toward the "house". As he pushed his way through the front door, he heard the jingling of

Sugar's tags at the rear towards the bedroom.

"Honey, I'm home," he laughed as he took his shoes off and placed them beside the door. He heard Sugar's paws hitting the floor as she jumped down from whatever piece of furniture she had been laying on. Wyatt continued through the breezeway into the living room but froze in the doorway for a second before backing up to the monitor just above him on the wall. He stared at it intently for a few minutes before reacting.

"What the..."

Wyatt moved as close to the monitor as he possibly could, reaching up to adjust it so that he could see it at a better angle. He absent-mindedly scratched at his stubbly chin as he continued to stare at the monitor. After a minute, he reached down, never breaking his gaze, and palmed a wireless computer mouse. A small black arrow popped up on the monitor and moved toward the bottom right quadrant, opened a drop-down menu, and enlarged the view so that it now took up the entire monitor.

The afternoon sun was still hard at work shining above the empty driveway. It had snowed a few days prior but the cloudless sky and bare branches allowed for the sun to make light work of it, leaving only small patches here and there, mostly on grassy areas. The vast front lawn sported occasional heaps of snow, but the loose gravel drive had been clear for days. Before going underground, Wyatt had gone around the perimeter of the property setting little 'traps' that he would be able to see on the monitor and know that someone or something had been there. One type that he had used involved marking a young sapling with bright paint, tying a piece of fishing line at the top, bending it towards the ground without damaging it, and using the fishing line to anchor it, essentially making it a trip line that would, theoretically, release the sapling to its full height when tripped. In other areas, closer to the house, he had mounted solar powered, motion sensor floodlights. And in other places, he simply set up markers that would likely be disturbed by, yet unremarkable to, most people, such as piles of rocks or stacks of sticks set up in specific ways. None of these 'traps' were designed to hurt or detain the intruder, or even actively alert Wyatt to their presence. They were merely indicators to let him know that someone, or something, had been there. He hadn't really concerned himself too much with perimeter security. He didn't really expect anyone to survive above ground. But what caught his attention was an unintentional trap.

"That's weird," he said out loud. "I swear that's on the wrong side."

One day, when Sugar was still a puppy, Wyatt was walking with her as she explored the large property. It was autumn at the time and she was having fun sniffing around and jumping into the natural drifts of leaves. Wyatt was hysterical watching her, as she would spot a pile of leaves and then drop onto her front elbows as if stalking it before running full speed and leaping into it headfirst. She would bounce back out a second later, shaking her head with a big goofy grin as she shook the leaves from her. A particularly large drift had formed under the biggest tree on the property, an old white oak. Sugar bounded toward it and leapt into the pile near the base of the tree. Wyatt was still laughing as she disappeared beneath the blur of oranges, reds, and browns. After a few seconds, Sugar still had not resurfaced and the leaves settled back into a calm, unmoving pile. Wyatt stopped laughing and ran over to the tree. Just as he reached spot where she had disappeared, he noticed a flicker

34

of movement in the leaves. He reached in and put one hand on Sugar to calm her while frantically brushing leaves out of the way. As he worked, he realized that she had gotten one of her front legs caught in a tangle of roots above the ground. He focused on calming her and got her to lay down after a minute, at which point he gently pulled her paw from its trap. Luckily, she hadn't been hurt in the incident, only frightened. Not wanting to disturb the roots of such a large, old tree, Wyatt removed the red bandana from his vest pocket and tied it onto the lowest branch nearest to the driveway, where he would be sure to see it so they could avoid a similar fate in the future.

As Wyatt stared at the monitor, he could see the red bandana tied to the lowest branch of the old white oak tree. His concern was over the fact that the red bandana was now tied around the lowest branch on the opposite side, closer to the fence at the edge of the property. Wyatt examined the other three screens for any indications that a trespasser had been through but found nothing else. Eventually, he returned the screen to its original view and stepped back.

"Why would someone do that?" Wyatt wondered aloud as he grabbed the mouse and began another marathon of menus. He was hoping to catch the trespasser in the recorded footage and wishing he had opted for more than the minimum package, which only saved the footage for an hour before erasing it. The idea was that an hour should be enough time to back up the footage should an incident occur, but Wyatt hadn't really thought he would be alone in the bunker. He had planned for someone to be available to check the feed every hour. As Wyatt reached the beginning of the video, he found that he was not that lucky. The bandana remained in place, in the wrong place.

He returned the screen to its original view before walking over to the couch and sitting down. Sugar, who had been watching from the kitchen, came over and climbed onto the couch next to him. He removed his wristwatch and started fiddling with the buttons. The first one he pushed illuminated the face with a washed out green glow. The next button changed the display, cycling through the time, date, and alarm clock. Finally, when Wyatt pressed the third button, the display began to blink. He pressed the button repeatedly until he found the chime option, turning it on so it would beep every hour and remind him to check the surveillance cameras. He let the display blink until it reset itself to the current time, then put it back on his wrist.

"Maybe it's a signal from mom and dad," he said as he scratched behind Sugar's ears.

Wyatt held out hope that his parents had made it somewhere safe. He had tried desperately to get them to join him in the bunker but they refused, insisting that everything was fine. He knew that the chances of them making it through everything were slim, but the thought of them perishing along with most of the population was something that he wasn't ready to accept. Wyatt knew that there were other bunkers and safe places closer to their home that they could have gone to, but he was also aware of just how stubborn his parents could be. If his father truly believed that there was no threat and that they weren't in imminent danger, nothing would convince him to go underground. They had tried to persuade him to come and stay with them at their home a few counties away, again insisting that there was no reason to enter the shelter, but Wyatt was as stubborn as his dad.

Sugar slowly made her way down to the floor and stretched out alongside the couch as Wyatt turned and put his feet up where she had been laying. He had completely forgotten about

36

lunch as he thought about his parents. He usually tried not to think about his family and friends too much, as it was depressing to think of what horrible fates they had likely met, but this time he couldn't help it. He replayed snippets of old memories as he tried to figure out who would be the type of person that would move a bandana from one tree branch to another, and what that action itself could mean. He could think of a few people that might do something like that knowing it was the type of thing Wyatt would notice right away, therefore alerting him to the fact that someone had made it to his house. But he could also think of a couple of people that might have been sending some type of threatening message with it. It was also entirely possibly, he reasoned, that it was a completely random survivor who did it out of boredom or because they thought it was funny. The possibilities were abundant and as he played through several of them in his head, Wyatt and Sugar both drifted to sleep.

Sleeping in the bunker had never been satisfying. Restful nights did not come easy when your dreams were teeming with tsunamis chasing down your parents, nuclear bombs obliterating your brother's entire city while you watch helplessly as it streams online, unfamiliar armies marching down your street, armed to the teeth and ready to avenge hundreds of years of oppression and abuse by your people, and any number of other things the mind conjures up in times of high stress. It didn't help that Wyatt was an avid reader of science fiction, zombie apocalypse, and dystopian novels. Nightmares had plagued him since the first night underground.

Wyatt was in the middle of one of these vivid dreams when he was jolted awake by his mother's voice. He knew that it must have been part of the dream, but the realness startled him. He sat up and rubbed his eyes, hoping for clarity. He thought back to when he was a boy and his mother would wake him for school, and how it had always taken him a few minutes longer than his brother to shake off the confusion of transitioning from sleeping to awake. Having always had an overactive imagination, it was sometimes difficult for him to distinguish what was dream and what was reality. As a tactic to help sort it out, he had developed a habit over the years of talking himself through the process out loud. While Wyatt's family had grown to see this coping mechanism as just another one of his many eccentricities, they were alarmed when he had first started doing it. His mother worried that he was talking to imaginary friends or ghosts, but his father, always more focused on the physical world, worried that he was talking to himself. His father was right, of course. Wyatt was talking to himself, however, not in the way that his father thought. It was, in his mind, more of a fill-in-the-blank questionnaire that he had come up with to ground himself.

"I dreamed about _____. But it can't be real because _____."

As Wyatt would answer the questions in his head, he would often whisper the responses out loud repeatedly until he was sure he believed it. When his parents asked him about this new behavior, he had told them that it helped him figure out what was real and what wasn't, but he didn't elaborate much because he didn't know how to explain beyond that. As he developed other quirks over the years, they dragged him to psychiatrist, psychologists, general practitioners, neurologists, and any other doctor they thought might be able to explain his odd behavior, including a stint with a chiropractor that only lasted three appointments. They all said the same thing, though.

Wyatt seemed like a perfectly healthy and normal kid, just a little eccentric. They came to see these odd behaviors as yellow flags to be noted instead of red flags to be observed constantly.

"It can't be mom because mom didn't make it," he whispered to himself, opening his eyes. "It was just a dream."

He looked at the floor beside the couch to see that Sugar was no longer there. He jumped up and was about to call out for her when he saw that she was laying against the storage closet just beyond the corner of the wall, barely out of sight from where he had been on the couch. He let out a sigh of relief as he started walking over to her.

"Suge, you've got to stop doing that," he said, frustrated.

Sugar picked her head up and looked at him for a minute before sitting upright, but made no effort to move.

"You want to get something to eat? I'm pretty hungry," he continued. "I completely missed lunch. It's almost dinner time now."

Wyatt began to cross the room towards the kitchen, but stopped when he saw that Sugar had not moved from her spot by the storage closet. He shook his head and continued across the room. When he reached the kitchen, he opened the cabinet beside the fridge, pulled down an airtight container filled with vacuum-sealed, single serve packages of noodles and removed one labeled 'Rigatoni'. He resealed the container and put it back in the cabinet before closing the door and opening the next cabinet door. After digging around for a couple of minutes, Wyatt found what he was looking for, a plain 16 oz can with a handwritten label that read 'Marinara' followed by a date. He closed the cabinet and placed the items on the counter beside the stove, then grabbed two small saucepans from the dishrack and filled one with water before placing them on the stovetop.

As the water heated, Wyatt grabbed a small jar of Vienna sausages from the cabinet, twisting the lid until he heard a satisfying pop. He removed two, sliced them, and mixed them into Sugar's bowl of kibble before closing the jar and placing it in the refrigerator. He placed the bowl on the floor, then rinsed and refilled her water bowl with fresh water, before calling her.

"Sugar, dinner time."

Sugar sat up and looked at him but didn't move. Wyatt picked up the food bowl and held it out so she would see the sausages mixed in, still she remained seated on the breezeway floor. He shook the bowl from side to side, hoping the noise would stir her, but it didn't. Instead, she turned her attention to the monitor and radio in front of her and laid back down.

"Okay," Wyatt sighed as he put the bowl back on the floor. "I get it. I'll leave it here for now in case you change your mind."

He turned his attention back to his own food, pouring the rigatoni into the newly boiling water and lowered the heat under the sauce until it was barely on. He stirred the pasta for a few seconds to keep it from sticking, then quickly walked over into the living room, from where he could see the monitor in the breezeway. Nothing out of the ordinary, other than the red bandana he had noticed earlier. He glanced at Sugar before returning to the stove. He decided to stay in the 'house' with her for the rest of the day and keep an eye on her. He was worried that she might not be feeling well, which could indicate several issues ranging from something as simple as her breakfast giving her gas or something as potentially catastrophic as air filtration or water filtration problems.

Wyatt considered the possibilities as he turned off both burners and carried the saucepan with the pasta in it to the sink. As he drained the water out, he heard the jingling of Sugar's tags as she suddenly jumped up and let out a single, loud bark. It had been so long since he had heard her at full volume that he jumped out of fright, dropping the pasta into the sink, and shouted, "Holy sh– Sugar!"

Sugar turned to look at Wyatt as he picked the strainer full of noodles from the sink before letting out another loud woof. Wyatt poured the pasta from the strainer back into the saucepan and set it down on the counter. Sugar had begun pacing the breezeway, giving off a low, constant grumble mixed with an occasional high-pitched whine. Wyatt turned and headed toward her, assuming he would look at the surveillance monitor and see some wild animal on one of the screens. It hadn't happened often, but there had been a few occasions when Sugar had gotten excited about something on the screen and reacted the same way. But as he closed the distance, he heard the unmistakable crackle of his ham radio speaker.

"Wyatt? Wyatt, can you hear me?"

He froze when he heard the voice coming from the speaker. It wasn't possible.

"Wyatt, please respond if you can hear me."

"Mom?" Wyatt whispered to himself. "But.. mom!"

He desperately wanted to pick up the radio and answer her, yet he couldn't will himself to move. He had spent months convincing himself that there was no way that his family could have survived the events of that day. He immediately became uneasy, suspecting that it was some type of trick to get to him, his bunker, or his supplies. Sugar barked once more, breaking Wyatt's concentration.

"Wyatt, if you can hear me, it's mom. Your father and I have been trying to reach you. We're really worried about you." She paused, and it sounded to Wyatt as though she was sniffling.

"Dad is on his way up there to come get you," she continued. "You need to go with him. We made an appointment with a psychiatrist. It's first thing in the morning. Dad will keep Sugar with him in the car," she paused again briefly, letting out a big sigh before going on. "Wyatt, you need to go. This has gone way too far. You need help. Dad says he'll call the police to break the door down if he has to."

Just then, Wyatt heard a loud banging on the steel security door. Sugar took off running toward the door, barking like mad.

"Wyatt, baby, can you hear me?" She was crying into the mic now. "Please, just pick up the mic and let me know you're okay."

"Wyatt," a deep, masculine voice called out from behind the door. It sounded as though he was a mile away. "Wyatt, this is Officer Doyle. I'm with your father. Open the door, son."

Author Bio

Jack Appell is an emerging author of short stories from the Charlotte, NC area who has appeared in several anthologies and currently has several projects in the works.

Find his work on Amazon at http://amazon.com/author/authorjackappell

Connect with him on Facebook at https://m.facebook.com/AuthorJackAppell/

DEREK SHUPERT

A Werewolf Hunter Short Story

LYCAN RISING

ONE

Blood is thicker than water.

That's what Pop use to say to Dean and me when we'd go at it. Our fights were always stupid, and generally involved some girl that we were competing over. What started out as heated words always escalated to a knock out fist fight. Two black eyes later, a busted lip, and broken nose, Pop would step in and finally break it up.

He didn't care much for the petty squabbles that young men have. There were more important matters to attend to. Like slaying lycans.

"You two knuckle heads need to get your heads out of your asses and focus on real world problems. Not this frivolous bickering and alleyway brawling that you're doing. The fight isn't here, but out there. If we lose focus and slip for just a single second, then those furry bastards win. All this, our way of life, is over." He'd pause for a split second, and let us chew on his wisdom.

At the time, it seemed annoying, and I didn't want to hear it. Just more jargon from the stern father that kept us in line. Although bitter to the taste, we digested his message without even knowing it.

"Just remember boys, in the end, when your backs are against the wall and the world is bearing down on you, you've got each other. Don't forget that."

Pop had a way with words, and putting life into a perspective that really brought it all together. In the end, I think he'd be proud of what Dean and I have accomplished, and what I had to do.

"Nathan, you ok, bro?"

I cut my eyes to the right, layers of tears coating the redness of my pupils. Scott stands there, his bulk resting against the aged white door frame. He says not another word, holding any further small talk until I reply. But to be honest, I don't know how to respond. My bloodline is all but gone. Extinguished by the evil that now plagues this desolate and defunct planet.

"It wasn't your fault, Nathan. How were you suppose to know that Thorin was baiting you into a trap? There's always a risk when we go out and hunt. You know this and so does Dean."

"Because it is my job to know!" I press down hard on the sink's edge, snapping it free from the deteriorated wall. I toss it to my left, breaking the grungy basin into chunks of useless rubble. "Dean is dead. Why do you persist on speaking as if he's still here, huh?"

Scott stands up straight, a look of remorse flooding his face as I point to Dean's headless corpse resting against the far wall. Blood pools under his body, coating the checkered linoleum floor in a dark red hue. Scott rubs his massive hands up and down his face as his eyes glaze over. I know what he was trying to say, but the festering guilt that is burrowing deep inside my soul won't let me go. Won't leave me be.

"I'm sorry, man. I didn't mean it like that."

"My brother is dead. Gone. Never to return." My eyes glaze over with sadness, and my hands tremble as I bring them up in front of me. Dean's blood is still smeared all over my palms, the fresh stench of lycan still lingering in the air. It makes my nose crinkle and distort as I catch a whiff of something foul. My stomach rumbles and acts as though it may release its contents at any moment. That's when my tongue finally manages to speak the words. "I killed my brother. My kin."

Scott gently places his hand on my right shoulder. My focus is on the blood—Dean's blood. It's gripping me tight and won't let me go. No matter how much I try to pull away, I can't. My gaze wants to look over at his body, but Scott stops me by subtly shaking my shoulders.

"You listen to me. Regardless of what you think, you did the right thing. The only thing you could do. Dean told you as much. He didn't want to turn and become part of Thorin's pack. We've all made that agreement. No matter how hard it may be, we take care of our own."

I take a deep breath and hold it before exhaling slowly through my quivering lips. Scott is right, whether I want to admit it or not. Thorin is to blame for all of this. For how this world is now. He is a plague that has been unleashed upon man, killing everyone and everything. He must be stopped once and for all. Regardless of my fate, I will make sure that happens.

"You good now, bro?"

"Yeah. Thanks." I lift my weary head and give Scott a reassuring nod as he pats my shoulder. I brush my arm across my face, wiping away the tears streaming out of my eyes. Scott does much the same as he burrows his thumb and index finger into the glistening wetness of his eyes. The discord that resides in me hasn't been resolved, but it has been tabled until there is time to fully grieve.

"What's the play here, brother? However you want to deal with this, I'm down. Thick or thin, I got your back till the end."

Scott takes a step back to give me some space. I erase the sadness from my face, and hone my thoughts once more. I need to be focused, free of any emotion or distractions that will hinder my judgement. It's so incredibly hard, but I fight through the hurt and pain.

"We load up and go after him with everything we've got. If we cut the head off the snake, then the body will die. His pack will scatter, and discord will run through the rest of his lycan brethren," I say with an emotionless tone.

"How do we find him?" Scott inquires as he laces his thick arms across his broad chest. "He's always moving, jumping from place to place."

"We go ask our guest politely where he is."

TWO

Scott is gracious enough to take care of Dean's body for me. I told him numerous times that I would handle it, but he wasn't having it. He kept telling me to leave him be, and get started on tracking down Thorin. He will give Dean the proper burial he deserves. Once it is done, he'll let me know.

Not sure what we did to deserve having Scott cross our path somewhere around five years ago. My sense of time is all but irrelevant in this dark age. At the time, it was almost as if fate knew our destinies were intertwined. A badass hunter if there ever was one, Scott was a one-man lycan-slaying machine. We were fortunate to have him join us as a hunter. But more importantly, we were grateful to have gained another brother.

Working my way down the rickety, metal spiral staircase to

the basement, the sounds of struggle and shouting meet my ears. Growls and snarls, more beast-like than man, grow louder as I near the bottom. The demonic noise does little to sway my emotions. My intent and resolve are sound, and soon, this lycan trash will learn the meaning of pain.

I give but a moments pause at the reinforced steel door, checking to make sure the weakness that was flowing from my eyes has all been extinguished.Although the fragments of my pain and anguish are not fully erased, I need to make sure this animal doesn't smell the stench of loss lingering in my soul.

I inhale a big draw of air and hold briefly, before exhaling it out through my stern and rigid lips. My eyes narrow, brows slanted inward as the suffering consuming me turns to bitter contempt and rage for the vile furry beasts. I'm ready to interrogate.

Moving the handle down, I pull the hefty door toward me. The hinges squeak, fighting through the decades of rust coating them. The pungent odor of the lycan, chained to the far wall hits me like a freight train. My nose wrinkles from the stifling stench. The wild animal turns my way.

"Fight, strain, growl, and snarl as much as you wish. You're not going to break free from those chains." I slam the door behind me, making sure it's latched. I have this bastard dead to rights, and he isn't leaving this room until I extract what I need from him. Well, not alive anyways.

The muscles in the lycan's chest and stomach flex and tighten. His massive arms press the chains and the plates that are bolted to the wall behind him to the brink of snapping. His bear like paws fidget and move as he continues his useless campaign. The chains hold strong despite his efforts. Thick strings of saliva drip from his short black snout. His teeth glisten from the lone overhead light that frames the beast in such a dramatic, terrifying portrait.

"Fine. Don't listen to me. Tire yourself out. Might make this infinitely easier on me." I retrieve a beat up old folding chair from the wall to my right and place it directly in front of the lycan. I causally sit down, and fold my arms across my chest. In this time of sorrow and mourning, I am finding a hint of joy watching the beast fight to break the chains that bind him.

He gives one last deep growl as his large yellow eyes bear down on me. He tilts his head up toward the ceiling and howls. Looking back down at me, his body begins to change back to his human form.

The dark black fur coating his body gives way to tan skin. His elongated boney-clawed paws shrink down to that of an average size man. His snout recedes and his face conforms back to a human. He screams in agony, the transformation brutal and unbearably painful. He closes his eyes for a brief moment before opening them back to his normal shade of auburn.

He grunts and groans, his chest heaving in and out as he spits a wad of saliva and blood off to the side. His fangs recede back into his jaw. His eyes deadlock on mine and a sinister smirk creeps across his sweaty face. I toss him a pair of ratty denim jeans.

"I'm glad you finally came to see me, Nathan. It was getting so lonesome down here by myself," he says calmly as he regains control of his exacerbated breathing. He slips on the jeans, his wicked gaze staying with me. "I see from the blood on your hands and the guilt in your eyes, you had to put Dean down. Such a pity and waste really. Thorin would've welcomed him into the pack with open arms. You as well."

Aryn, one of Thorin's more experienced sentinels, has been with Thorin for as long as I can remember. We've managed to take out a few others, but Aryn has always eluded us.

Until now.

I do not entertain Aryn's comment, brushing it off as useless banter as my gaze holds firm and strong. His body relaxes. His arms fall to his sides as he leans back against the dark reddish-brown brick wall. The smirk remains on his smug face, though.

"Dean's at rest now. At peace. He no longer has to deal with the likes of your kind," I snidely remark.

"I imagine it was painful for you to take his head. Almost like losing a part of yourself. Your soul becoming detached from your own body and afterwards, you're nothing more than an empty vessel. Hollow and cold."

"Then we share some common ground." I lean forward in my chair, clasping my hands in front of me as I keep my emotionless gaze fixed upon him.

Aryn chuckles, snickering under his breath as he digs his fingernail between his teeth. Such arrogance. "As much as I've enjoyed our small talk, Nathan, why don't you tell me what you want? I highly doubt you came down here to BS with me."

"Thorin. Where is he?" I flatly ask.

"Oh, Nathan. Are you sure you want to travel down that road again? I mean, you just lost your brother on such a fool's errand. Now, you're all alone."

"Just answer the question," I hiss. "I know that isn't the only hideout he has in the city. Once a den is compromised, you move to the next. Then the next. So, again, where has Thorin gone?"

"Man. I can see why he wants you and your brother. Such tenacity. Such will for vengeance. He has plans for you, you know. Just like your brother. You could easily become his Beta. His second in command. In time, of course. You would have to suspend your campaign of trying to slay our kind, though. As much as he would like to convert you, Nathan, he will kill you without pause if you continue down this path."

"The only plan I have that concerns Thorin is relieving his body of his head. Rid this planet of the pestilence you lycan's have infected it with." I snarl. "Now tell me where he is, and perhaps, I'll provide you with a quick death."

"There is nothing you can threaten me with, Nathan. Death is but a mere stepping stone to another existence," Aryn leans back against the rigid brick wall and smiles at me. "Here's some friendly advice, seeing as soon you'll either be turned and be part of the pack or dead. Let me go and allow what is destined to happen, happen. You can't fight it. You can only accept it."

I nod my head. Although having Aryn cooperate would make this go much smooth, I was hoping for the rockier path. I've got some aggression and stress I need to vent to get my mind right.

Standing up from my chair, I stare at Aryn. The arrogance of his kind is astounding.

"We're not done already, are we, Nathan?" Aryn inquires. "I feel as though we are bonding here. Getting some good one on one time before you join the pack."

I walk over to the cabinet against the wall behind me, and open the aged oak doors, revealing my father's double-headed battle axe. I grab its thick, dark cherry wooden handle, and lift it free from the two metal hooks in the center of the cabinet.

It's been ages since I've last held it. It's as light as air. My eyes gleam over of the blade itself. Aryn is still running his mouth, but I ignore him as I soak in the precision of both of the bits.

The entire head of the axe is completely made of silver. This was Pop's trusted weapon. He used it on every hunt. He left it to Dean and myself. Said it was good luck, but to be honest, we couldn't bear to use it. After all, it was Pop's. Too many memories. We wanted to retire it. Considering recent events though, I could use some good luck.

"Do you know what's hard to manage? I mean, really hard to handle during times of extreme duress? When you're under so much pressure, and your mind feels like it's being ripped in half over and over again?" I turn swiftly around, my gaze cutting to Aryn as I lean the handle against my right shoulder.

"What is that, Nathan?"

"Hate." I walk toward him, that smug expression still plastered on his face as if he's in complete control and doesn't have anything to worry about. I plan to erase that. "It's the kind of vindictive vengeance that starts here, in the pit of your gut, where it stirs and boils like hot lava. Then it rises fast and volcanic, erupting hot on your breath. Your eyes then go wide with fire and you clench your teeth so hard you think they might shatter like glass."

"Can't say that I have felt that, Nathan." Aryn grins.

"Yeah. Me neither." I remove the axe from my shoulder and jam the head into Aryn's throat. I shove him hard against the wall, pressing with all my might. Like a branding iron to a cows hide, smoke plumes from the contact as he squirms along the rigid brick wall façade. Man. As if his kind didn't smell already, the burning of his skin is foul.

He writhes in pain, trying to grab the head of the axe and push it away. His hands smoke just as his fangs begin to show. His eyes go wide, and that yellow tint floods his irises. Thick streams of white saliva spew from his lips as he grits his teeth.

"Not so smug now, are you?" I snarl as I dig the head of the axe deep into his throat, choking him. "Where is Thorin at?"

"I... don't... know!" Aryn cries out through the pain.

"Where is he?" I lift up with all my might, pressing the axe upwards. I lift him slightly off the ground as the stench of burning flesh fills my nose.

"Okay!" Aryn cries out in pain. "Just get this off me!"

I remove the head of the axe as he drops to the floor with a thud. His singed hands clasp his throat as he takes in big gulps of air.

"All talk and no bite, huh. I thought there wasn't anything I could threaten you with. Pathetic." I place the bit close to his chin and he flinches and falls back against the wall. "I can't tell you how many of your kind my father slayed with this axe. Too many to count, I imagine. So much lycan blood this tormentor of the damned has spilled. And you know what, it's still as sharp as ever."

"I can tell you... where he'd probably... head next." Aryn's chest heaves out, then in. The words sputter from his lips with such struggle that it almost brings a smug smirk to my face. "There are multiple places he could retreat to, but this is his favorite. If I tell you, will you let me go?"

I kneel down to his level, the battle axe resting on my leg as he glances up at me. The wicked burn mark on his throat is raw, the skin blackened with spots of red throughout. In time, it will heal as if it never happened.

"Tell me where Thorin is, and you have my word, I will release you."

"South side of town. The Old Glory Distillery." I stand back up as Aryn's gaze follows me. He lifts his shackled arms into the air. "We had a deal. Now, release me, Nathan."

"You are right, and I am a man of my word." I pull the axe back over my shoulder and lop Aryn's head off. No hesitation. His arms plummet to his sides as his body slumps over to the left. The expression captured on his face as the blade meets his flesh is that of a distant stare. Although, I would attest that he probably knew it was coming. One less lycan in this god forsaken world.

"You're released."

THREE

The sadness I'm feeling has morphed and changed. My mind is honed now, fixed on the mission I have before me. No weakness. No mercy. Just a clear understanding that no matter what, Thorin is going to die by my hand.

I leave Aryn's headless body still shackled and slumped over. Pop's battle axe stays within my grasp as I open the steel door and head upstairs to the armory. My thick-soled boots hit the aged, scuffed-up oak floor. I march down the long hallway, the frail planks creaking under my bulk as I hang a left.

I give but a moments pause to take in the periphery of the war room. Steel cages cover every inch of the condemned space we're holed up in. Filled with an array of battle axe's, knives, crossbows, firearms, and silver bullets, it is never hard to find what we need to handle the job.

Dean always used the right side of the room, Scott the middle, and I took the left. When we came in here to gear up for a hunt,

Dean would always put on some old school, heavy metal music that would rattle your teeth inside your skull. Seemed to get us pumped up.

My mind wants to wander to those moments we shared in the war room, but I stay the thoughts and head over to my table. I can't get distracted again. Not now. There's too much at stake. Got to keep my focus on the mission.

I plop Pop's battle axe on the metal table in front of my area. I swing open the steel cage's doors, and retrieve the rucksack that is nestled at the bottom. I place it next to the axe and unzip it. I turn sharply around, and begin pulling free any and all weapons that I can carry.

There are many to choose from, but I start with the crossbow and two 9mm pistols. I place them methodically on the table as I go back for the bows and boxes of silver bullets.

"What's going on?" Scott inquires as he comes over to the table. "Did Aryn give up Thorin's location?"

"In a manner of speaking," I flatly respond. Scott brushes off the cold, blunt response with a simple nod as his gaze diverts down to the bloodied bit of the axe. "The Old Glory Distillery. Not sure if he's full of crap or what, but I'm going to check it out regardless."

"Sounds like you got some answers, then. And perhaps, some closure?"

"He gave me what I asked for. I returned the favor in kind."

I load the silver bullets into one magazine after another till they're filled to capacity. Scott stands there, silent as he watches me plan for what I can only assume he thinks is a suicide mission. I keep my eyes on the task at hand, not giving him the opportunity to offer his insight.

"Listen, Nathan, I—"

"If you're going to try and talk me out of going, I wouldn't waste your breath. This is going to happen." I slap a magazine into each of the pistols, then take a handful of the magazines and stuff them into the rucksack. I leave the others on the table.

"Actually, I wasn't."

I pause what I'm doing and glance over to Scott. He's resting both of his hands on top of the table. His long, saddened gaze looms in my direction. There's a mixture of emotions on his face: Hate. Anger. Loss. And everything else that I'm struggling with as well.

"Really? Doesn't seem like you to not be the voice of reason."

"We're lycan hunters. If we catch wind of a den, then we handle it. That's what we do. Enough said." Scott doesn't bat an eye. In the past, he has always been the hesitant one. Wanting to dissect every possible outcome that could potentially arise. To say this is out of character for him is an understatement.

"So, why no objections?" I raise my right brow slightly. "I was expecting you to come over and give me the third degree. Tell me I'm emotional and not thinking clearly. Perhaps I need to deal with the passing of Dean first before rushing out into another fight."

"Don't get me wrong, we need to be smart about how we approach this. I've lost one brother. I don't plan on loosing another," Scott replies sincerely but tactfully. "I want Thorin just as bad as you do. We have both suffered and lost so much because of him and his kind. If we have the chance to take him out once and for all, then I'm all in."

"Not what I was expecting to be honest." I turn to my right and fetch a handful of throwing knives, made out of silver, and place them on the table.

"Yeah well, I got your back, brother. No matter what. We

finish this together or die trying."

"I appreciate that."

Scott offers a simple nod as he places his hand on my right shoulder. I return the gesture, feeling more confident now.

"When are we rolling out?" Scott asks.

"Just as soon as you get your gear together," I respond.

"Copy that." Scott makes a beeline for his section of the armory. He wastes little time gathering up his tools of the trade. To say that I'm a bit relieved by his actions is an understatement. I was going to do this regardless of what he said, but I'm glad he has my back.

We both finish rounding out our armament, stuffing our rucksacks to the brim. I grab my utility belt and fill each slot with as many magazines as I can. I place it around my waist, and snap it into place, then load the throwing knives into the sheath that is attached to my upper right thigh.

Scott stands by the doorway, fully decked out in weaponry. He's always prepped and ready to move out before everyone else. I've never been as efficient as him. Perhaps I should take heed of his actions.

I rest the crossbow and Pop's battle axe on top of the rucksack. My fingers wrap around the tattered brown handle and lift it free from the table's surface. Its bulk tugs at my arm as I walk over to Scott, who glances down briefly.

"Bringing your dad's axe, I see."

"Yeah. Hoping for some good luck for a change," I respond with a nod.

"Didn't bother to clean off Aryn's blood, huh?" Scott bends down and retrieves his gear from the floor.

"Nah. Thought I'd leave it. Let those lycan's smell their fallen brethren from the tip of their soon to be reaper."

Scott slings his rucksack over his right shoulder as he turns to walk out of the armory. He pauses briefly, tilting his head to the left. "You sure about doing this now? I'm with you either way, Nathan. Just making sure is all."

"I am."

Scott offers a single nod and moves on. He heads down the hallway to the right. I trail behind him as we make our way to the stairwell. We make short work of the four flights of stairs and enter the cramped, dismal garage of the building.

It's cold, dark, and silent. The musty stench of the enclosed space crinkles my nose as the steady drip of water plays in my ears. A lone light dangles from the rafters overhead like a hangman's noose. It subtly glides to and fro, as if the breath of death itself is making its presence known. Foreshadowing our fate? Possibly. But currently, I could care less. After I'm finished with Thorin, then we can hash out the afterlife.

"Your ride or mine?" Scott stops before our respective abominations that we call war riders.

Looking at the ragtag bunch of rusted steel and mismatched panels, you'd think we had some sort of mad scientist working on the vehicles. In a way, we do.

Each rider is held together by whatever we can scavenge. There are a smorgasbord of abandoned cars, trucks, and other big rigs that are wasting away in the remnants of a world that would never restore their bodies to their former glory. Dean and I knew enough about cars to get us by. Scott, on the other hand, is a diabolical genius.

"Let's take yours," I respond with a tilt of my head. "Might need the extra horsepower and four-wheel drive. Don't think the Charger would be a good fit for this hunt. Besides, I might need the room. Trophies."

"Sounds good. The beast has got roughly a half tank or so. We should be good to go." Scott heads over to the driver's side while I make for the passenger door. Truth be told, this garage would have a lot more room if we didn't have it stuffed with various car parts, tools, our vehicles, and other scavenged items that we have come across over the years. In a world where you can't just run to the store to get what you need, you keep everything you find. Better to be safe than regretful.

I stand on the tips of my toes as my fingers find the handle. I open the door and toss my rucksack up onto the floorboard. I scale the side of the truck like a mountain climber, plopping down onto the cracked leather seats that have the cushions showing through in places. Despite the outwardly drab appearance of Scott's war rider, he's done remarkably well with keeping it in top running condition. After all, they aren't built for show.

He goes to start the beast, but pauses. With his right hand, he digs into his brown cameo cargo pants and fishes something out. He glances my way while holding out his hand. "Thought you might want this."

I hold my hand out, palm facing up as he places Dean's dog tags in my grasp. I bring the metal-plated disc closer and read the inscription.

May my courage and resolve be stronger than that of my enemy. For the forces of good will trump the wicked.

Dean was a skillful master of taming words in a way that I never could. A wicked tongue when need be, but also so prolific. Damn, I miss him.

"Thanks. I appreciate this."

"Not a problem."

I place the tags around my neck as Scott turns the engine over. It grumbles at first, idling rough as the entire cab shakes and vibrates. He pumps the gas pedal a few times, revving the engine till it toes the redline. He continues for a few more seconds, applying the gas and letting off till it levels out.

"A little mood music?" he inquires with a glance my way.

I nod. "For Dean."

Scott turns on the radio and cranks the volume up. The speakers hum with anticipation as he puts the war rider into reverse. The subtle symphony of music filters out through the dash and door speakers as a guitar solo grows louder. This was one of Dean's favorite bands to listen to while hunting. Always seemed to get him in the right frame of mind. Seems only fitting that we have it playing now.

I glance out the grimy window, my gaze looming in the darkness as the music continues its rhythmic intensity. Scott taps his fingers on the steering wheel as he comes to a halt. He puts the beast into drive and punches the gas. The squeal of the tires bounces off the walls and echo throughout the garage as we take off.

We make a beeline for the exit. The truck drops forward, racing down the decline toward a brick wall. Scott torques the wheel hard to the right, sending the bulky rig into a power slide. The tires continue their banshee screams as he expertly maneuverers the darkness without fault.

He straightens out the beast and hits the gas. There's daylight seeping in through the boarded-up windows ahead, the bleakness of the darkness trying to fend off the strident sunshine.

The truck explodes out onto the abandoned streets as the

61

metal music fills the cab. Scott brings the rig back under submission as we rip down the street and head for Thorin's den.

FOUR

After about the fourth song, I reach over and turn the volume down. Scott's fingers continue to play along the steering wheel as he maneuvers the congested city streets. He doesn't bat an eye at the parking lot of abandoned steel. He's traversed this city so many times I imagine he could probably do this blindfolded.

"Up here in a block or so, you're going to hang a right on Jefferson. Then you're-"

"I got you, Nathan." Scott cuts to the right, narrowly missing a military Humvee. We get up on the sidewalk, blowing past storefront after storefront that has been picked clean of anything of use. "Right on Jefferson then another three blocks down. The Old Glory Distillery is on the left."

"Have you been there before?" I inquire as I lift my right brow in curiosity.

"We've passed by it before. Actually, a few times." Scott gets us back on the street as the engine tames the silence that is now our world. "While you and Dean were strategizing and talking lycan shop, I made mental notes about landmarks and buildings we haven't cleared yet. Old Glory was one of them."

"Good to know." Just one more reason why Scott has been such an asset to us. "Any input on best entry points and such?"

"No clue, brother."

We take a right on Jefferson and Scott lets up on the gas. I lean forward in my seat, my eyes straining to peer down the street to the distillery. Massive cracks snake up the sides of the reddish brick structures. Portions of the walls are missing, rubble littering the sidewalks as weeds grow up through the disorder.

"How do you want to attack this?" Scott inquires as he pulls over to the left and stops the war rider.

As much as I'd like to have Scott drive the beast into the distillery and us go on a lycan killing spree, I table that plan. I'm still teeming with a fiery vengeance to slay any and all who get in my way, but I'm also hell bent on not letting Thorin slip through my fingers if he's here.

"We do it like we generally do any other den that we're investigating. You take the west side and I'll take the east. Kill anything with sharp claws and teeth. Did you bring your two-ways?"

"Yeah. Got'em stowed with the rest of my gear."

"Good. Go ahead and kill it. We'll go the rest of the way on foot."

Scott kills the engine and removes the keys from the ignition. We sit there for a minute, our gazes fixed on the distillery a block away. We're both icy calm, our demeanors without doubt or reservations. Even if we did, we were always good about hiding it from each other.

64

"You ready to do this?" Scott glances over at me.

"I'm ready to get my trophy."

Scott opens his door and stands on the railing that's attached to the side of his truck. He moves to the backseat as I grab my rucksack and follow suit. I jump to the ground below, move the battle axe and crossbow to the side, and unzip the resilient cordura made sack. Glancing at the contents inside, I second guess lugging the hefty weapons valet about as I hunt. I need to be light on my feet and not have anything that'll hinder my movement. When stuffing the bag full of extra magazines and such, I didn't think it would. Now, on the cusp of venturing into the lycan's den, I'm inclined to rethink that decision.

Screw it. I'll have to make every shot count.

I grab the crossbow and remove the magazine from the bottom. I know it's fully stocked, but my paranoia spurns me to check its capacity all the same. It's filled to the gills with twenty bolts that have silver tips attached to their ends. I've got two more magazines, stocked with as many bolts, stashed inside the rucksack, but they'll have to stay behind.

I snap the magazine back into place and slip the worn and tattered leather strap across my body. I dig out a few more magazines for the 9mm and stuff them inside the front of my pants.

"Channel two." Scott hands me one of the two-way radios along with a black earpiece. "Should be fully charged."

I take it from him and check to make sure it's on channel two. It is.

I place the M2 connector end into the headset jack, and slip the earpiece into my ear. "Testing. Testing."

Scott gives me a thumbs up as he clips his radio to his belt. He's got his rucksack slung over his shoulders, and his black tactical vest consumed with extra Berretta magazines. Clutched in his right hand, his stout battle axe rests against his shoulder.

"Be safe, brother, and watch your six."

"You as well."

I stand up straight and shake Scott's hand. We offer each other a simple nod before he turns and disappears around the front of the war rig. I finish out my last-minute skim of the contents inside the bag before deciding I'm good to go. I scoop up the handles and toss the bag inside the cab. Gently, I close the door and bend down to get Pop's axe. Clutching it tightly in my hands, my eyes cut over to the distillery.

Time to hunt.

I dash across the street that is littered with weeds sprouting up through the cracks in the concrete. My boots hit the sidewalk as I press my body flat against the building in front of me. I slowly slither down its course exterior. I pause just shy of the building's edge, and take in the derelict structure that's on the next block over.

From where I stand, it's hard to gauge if and where their sentries may be. If any. Aryn could've misdirected us away from Thorin, and sent me on a wild goose chase just to pour salt in my open wound. He knows how badly I want Thorin. Especially now that Dean has fallen because of him.

The sun starts its descent as large shadows consume the area. Darkness lingers behind the busted windows and open portions of the distillery. I bolt from the building's edge and dash across the street. The crossbow's bulk bounces against my back as I hit the east side of the building.

I grip the battle axe tighter as I take in a gulp of air. I exhale slowly through my nose to try and calm my nerves. It's not a sense of fear or terror that grips me so, but more a heightened state of readiness. I will exact my vengeance for Dean and be one step closer to ridding this world of the lycan plague.

Static fills my ears, followed by Scott's deep voice in a low whisper. "I'm in. Found an opening on the west wall. Over."

I take a few steps away from the building and glance to my right. There's a portion of the structure's wall that is missing.

"Copy that. Breaching shortly," I respond. "Anyone home? Over."

"Smells like it, but haven't gotten any visuals as of... wait a minute." Scott's breathing escalates.

I place my hand over my earpiece, and focus on every detail I can pick up. "What is it?" My heart pumps a tad faster. "Scott, what is going on in there? Do we have his den?"

Static abruptly fills my earpiece, the crisp crackling sound steady as I check the radio.

Come on, damn it.

Multiple howls spring up from within the structure, snaring my attention as my head shoots up toward the windows.

No, no, no...

I get down to the fissure in the wall. My hands brace against the busted brick as my boots rest on top of the rubble. Two deep and hard breaths escape my lungs as I start to enter the building, but pause at the static bleating from my side.

The radio comes back to life, fading in and out. There's commotion, as if its being jostled about with an unsteady hand.

"Scott. What's your status, over?" I frantically speak into the mic.

"I'm afraid your partner is currently indisposed."

My eyes widen at the familiar voice. A caldron of mixed emotions boils in the pit of my stomach as anger and rage wash over me like an ocean tide. I'm shocked, saddened, and relieved all at once.

"Thorin."

"Come inside, Nathan. We have a great many things to discuss, you and I. I'll be waiting for you."

The radio goes cold once more as I rip the earpiece from my ear. I'm foaming at the mouth, tears flooding my eyes as I pound my hands against the wall. Rage. It's such a hard emotion to control and contend with. But I must.

I duck and enter the building. My feet land on some steel grating. A catwalk. Holding the battle axe, I take in the expansive periphery of the distillery. There's a gaping hole in the center of the roof, allowing what little bit of the day's sunshine is left to bring light to the darkness within.

Massive rusted boiler pumps occupy the grounds like alien pods. Metal duct work slithers along the walls and the ceiling like a giant snake. The air reeks of lycan, the overwhelming foul stench of the unholy creature consuming the building.

Something moves within the pumps below, but it quickly disappears. I know it's a trap, but that doesn't deter me. I spot a set of stairs that lead down to the ground floor against the far wall. I head to the right at a brisk run. My boots play off the catwalk as I come to a junction up ahead. There're some steel lockers lining both sides as I crest the opening.

A large clawed hand swings at me, hitting me in the chest and knocking me back against the wall. The wind tears from my lungs, and my body bounces off the unforgiving surface. The crossbow does little to cushion the impact, its hard, metal construction digging into my back.

I collapse to one knee and my head tilts upward to the lycan who towers before me. Its yellow eyes draw me in as its putrid breath vents from its fanged muzzle. It advances.

Both hands grip the battle axe firmly. I strike the beast with an upward slash. The blade slices through its fur with ease, sending the creature reeling backwards. It paws at the open wound, blood leaking out. I lift the axe over my head and bring it down. The blade burrows into its thick skull, and it drops to its knees lifeless.

I pull the bit free and continue down the catwalk. When I spot two more lycans racing up the steel steps, I hang a left and make for the stairs. They hit the catwalk and head right for me. Without pause, I hurl the battle axe at the creature to my left. End over end, the weapon spins, finding its mark as it strikes the beast in the chest. I pull free my 9mm from its holster and open fire. The silver rounds impact the remaining lycan's chest, sending the brutish creature stumbling over the railing to my right.

Scooping up the axe, I move on to the stairs. My boots sound off on each step as I quickly race toward the ground floor. More movement catches my attention as their large frames coordinate within the maze of boiler pumps. I've seen Thorin only once in his animal state, much larger and more imposing than his pack members. If that's possible. I haven't come across him yet.

I slow my advancement, suck in a bit of air, and try to corral my thoughts. I can hear the creature's breathing within the maze of rusted steel, but cannot see them. One foot in front of the next, I move on.

The 9mm takes the lead, my right hand holding it steady as I train the barrel dead ahead. The axe rests in my left hand as I keep my head on a swivel. My eyes dart from side to side, scrutinizing every open space as my ears tingle from the creatures' heavy breathing.

Come on already. Attack me.

I afford a few more steps before they make me eat my words.

One attacks me from the right, swinging its massive arm at me. I duck down and roll head over heels, barely missing its clawed fingers. I get back upright, turn, and empty my clip in its chest as I lean back against one of the pumps. I eject the magazine, and pull a fresh one from my belt. I slap it into place, and load a round into the chamber. Something solid knocks me to the ground.

I slide across the floor and slam into one of the boiler pumps. The axe escapes my grasp as a lycan drops to all fours and comes at me. I unload two into its head, dropping it instantly. One advances to my left, galloping toward me. I extinguish the rest of the magazine trying to take it down. I eject the spent magazine and go for a fresh one.

A lycan emerges from the shadows to my right and grabs a handful of my shirt. I'm ripped off the dirt-covered floor. My feet leave the safety of the ground. I land shortly after with a hard thud.

I roll over and get to me knees. The 9mm is gone. I remove the crossbow from my back and take aim. My body throbs and aches, but I fight through the pain. I open fire, the compressed chambers expelling a sigh of air as the weapon sends a wave of silver-tipped bolts in the creature's direction. It manages to elude most of the arrows, shifting from side to side. A few strike it in its chest, causing the creature to stumble and howl in pain. I continue firing until the creature scurries off to my right, leaving my sight.

My right arm hurts from the jarring impact of slamming into the boiler pump. A deep pain bores into what seems like the bone marrow of my upper bicep. It's unrelenting, hurting like hell. I drop the spent crossbow to my side, and trudge back over in search of Pop's battle axe. I find it on the ground to my left, the handle sticking out between two boiler pumps.

Dropping the crossbow, I pick up the battle axe and come about. I make my way through the remainder of the boiler pumps without a lycan in sight. I come to an opening where I spot Thorin and Scott. Scott lays on his side with his back to me—motionless. Thorin stands off to his left with his foot resting on Scott's shoulder.

"Well, well, well, Nathan. You're not looking so hot," Thorin says with that ever-familiar smug smile his kind normally have. "To be honest, I'm a bit surprised that you made it this far. I had some of my best troops out after you."

"Yeah well, we have some business to discuss, you and I," I mutter back. Both of my hands wrap around the handle of the axe as my gaze hones in on Thorin. "I came for your head, and I'm not leaving without it."

"Here I am, Nathan. Give me your best shot." Thorin removes his foot from Scott's unconscious body. His tongue slithers out of his mouth, and glides around the edge of his lips as his eyes flash that yellow tint. I summon what strength I have left to slay the monster that has caused me so much pain.

For here in this moment, vengeance shall be mine.

Author Bio

Derek Shupert is an emerging Science Fiction Author known for his captivating dystopian storylines and post-apocalyptic-laden plots. With various books and anthologies underway, he is also the author of the Dead State series.

Find his books on Amazon at https://www.amazon.com/Derek-Shupert/e/B004XO8CX6

Bury Em' Deep by Stefan Lear

Joe hungrily eyed the lunch the waitress set on the table in front of him. On the plate was a pork chop that still sizzled from being seared on the grill and a large helping of mixed vegetables. His mouth watered.

"Thanks, Jennifer," he smiled and looked up at his server. "These look delicious."

"Don't eat so much that you don't have room for dessert. Bert made a special peach cobbler that even the dead would die for."

"I'll see if I can leave a little room. But if Bert keeps making my mouth water with just the main course I don't know if I can resist stuffing my face."

"Well see what ya can do. You know Bert gets upset when he bakes his specials and no one eats them. Besides, he gets cranky and I have to listen to his complaining."

"I'll do my best, Jen." Jennifer smirked and turned her attention to her other customers. As she walked away, Joe picked up his utensils and began devouring what promised to be a hearty meal.

After the last few days of chasing Derek Dark and his crew

he had built up an appetite. While he had been out with the other deputies the only thing he had eaten was flats and jerky. It wasn't gourmet food for sure, but it could sustain a man for weeks if that was the only thing to eat. Today, though, he would eat a proper meal. Derek closed his eyes and melted in his chair from the culinary cornucopia he chewed on.

I tried to open my eyes, but something pressed on them. I tried to open my mouth to say something, but dirt filled my throat silencing any sounds. What was going on? Where was I? The lack of air, the lack of sight, all of it made me angry. I tried to raise my arms, but something stopped me. That made me furious. I thrashed around; the rage growing. As I thrashed, whatever had me bound up grew looser and less restrictive.

My bonds gave way, my eyes flew open, and I spit dirt out of my mouth. Buried. Someone had buried me. I didn't remember what had happened. Questions swirled in my mind, but anger blotted them out. All I knew is rage and anger. Buried. They had buried me!

Suddenly another grave erupted and spewed forth its inhabitant. He spit dirt from his mouth just as another person breached the surface of their grave. And another person sat up not two feet away from them. All were spitting dirt. All seemed filled with anger. All had guns on their hips. I raised my face to the sky and screamed. Screamed forth my anger. Screamed forth my lust to kill whoever had put me in this grave. My scream was joined first by one, then by the other men that had resurrected and found an existence this side of the grave.

I struggled to stand. I regained my footing. I leaned back and raged at the sky, the other men watching me. Almost at once they stood up and joined my voice with theirs. Our voices pierced the sky, announcing to the world our arrival from the veil.

Some seminal part of me had reasoned that we had been dead, but it was a small voice buried deep inside a lost humanity. I felt feral. I needed to hunt, to hurt those that had done this to me. It was an instinct, a need to inflict pain. With that need came a hunger. It drove my actions. I grunted and set off toward town, the last place I had been. Town, where I last remembered being before I woke from death, spit out like a piece of rancid meat. The other men that had escaped the grave followed behind me. Our pace increased from a walk to a metered run.

"Honey, have you seen my sharpener?" Brandon asked.

"It should be on the top shelf, right next to the gun oil and the jar of lard," Jelena answered.

Brandon reached up to the shelf and moved the jar of lard to the side. Sure enough, there it was. He grabbed the oil and sharpener and walked to the table. He set them next to his swords. Both of them were sheathed in their scabbard.

"Make sure you disinfect that table after you clean your blades. I don't want any fungus among us. You never know if those damned spores are hitching a ride on something."

Brandon walked up behind his wife and hugged her around the waist. "I want to hitch a ride on you, Wifey."

Jelena turned around, Brandon's arm still encircling her, and smiled up at her husband. His charm and ruggedness never failed to make her smile. "You will not be riding anything but your horse if you don't clean up that table."

"Maybe Dasher would let me sleep with her in the barn."

"You and that horse: I swear you have a romance going on," Jelena smirked.

"Hmmm, we might. But you're my favorite. Besides, I was told you never get your honey where you get your money." Brandon broke his embrace and kissed his wife briefly. "Me and Dasher have a strictly business relationship."

He walked back to the table to begin cleaning his weapons, and Jelena turned back to the sink of dishes. "How did the hunt go? The rumors are that Derek Dark was a nasty, nasty man. He give you and the boys any trouble?"

"We caught them near in a canyon and boxed them in. It got hectic, but in the end, they got what they deserve. A bullet in the heart for each of them. Then we buried them all."

"Thank goodness. Lord knows they caused enough trouble in the territories. I'm glad they're gone."

"Don't worry, they won't be causing any more chaos except in hell." With those words, Brandon poured oil on one of the blades and began rubbing it. Jelena turned back to the dishes and began scrubbing.

"And if they do come back, we have something for them. Isn't that right," he silently asked his swords.

■ ◄ ▼

For half the day we ran. I didn't seem to tire. I didn't breathe hard, and I didn't sweat. Up the last hill we ran and there it was. That town, less than a hundred feet away now. The place my instinct drove me to. Driven by instinct, driven by rage, driven by hunger.

I stopped at the top of the hill and looked down on them. The anger burned in my chest, and I opened my mouth to discharge it toward the town's inhabitants. The men that traveled with me let loose their howls, too. It sounded like a pack of demon dogs angrily warning their prey of doom. Warning them of their death.

The people in the street jerked their heads up at the sound. All of us on the hill charged toward them. We ran down the hill, rage foaming through our teeth, snarling. Some screamed, others ran inside buildings. Some men, the ones that had guns, didn't run. They were our prey.

The men in the street pulled guns and started shooting at us. A bullet struck me in the chest. I heard the thunder of the report, felt the thud as it ripped into my chest. But I felt no pain, and no blood ran. I snarled and was slowed by the bullet. I regained speed and ran toward the one that shot me.

Instinctively I pulled my revolver from its holster and shot at him. The bullet found its mark and blood blossomed from the hole in his eye. The hunger burrowing in my gut took hold. I ran to the dead gunslinger and sank my teeth into his neck. I bit as hard as I could and ripped a chunk of flesh off. So good, so so good. I would feed. His flesh would sustain me.

Around me, chaos reigned as the other ones that ran with me found morsels to feast upon. The flesh didn't sate my hunger or my anger. I would need more after blood no longer flowed through this body. This is who I am, what I have become. Always more anger. Always more flesh. Always more blood.

■ ⋈ ▼

Joe was halfway into the delicious peach cobbler that Bert had cooked. It was delectable. It was good enough to present to the Gods.

Joe looked up and saw men and women running through the streets. Some women were screaming as they ran. The hairs on his neck rippled, and Joe stood immediately.

Cobbler forgotten, Joe reached for his scabbard and strapped his swords over his back. He reached down as he walked out the door and unsnapped his holster, giving him freedom to draw his guns if needed.

Joe looked the direction from which people were running. A shot rang out and a man was knocked to the ground, apparently hit. A figure ran to him and dropped down beside him. The figure raised his head, blood running down his jaw as he chewed.

Joe remained slack-jawed for only a fraction of a second. He then sprang into a full sprint toward the fallen man being gnawed upon. Joe drew his sword as he ran. He swung his sword as he reached the figure. The steel flashed in the sun, arcing in the air toward the neck of the kneeling man.

"Holy crap. That's Derek Dark!"

As the thought flashed through his mind, his sword hissed through the air and severed Derek's head from his body. The head arced through the air as Derek's body slumped to the ground. Joe looked up and saw the chaos caused by Derek's remaining crew.

He saw his coworker Brandon strolling down the street toward him. "It's Derek Dark's crew," he called to his friend. "The ground must have been bad where we buried them."

Brandon nodded his head in understanding. He holstered his gun and reached over his back. His hands grabbed the grips of his two swords and freed them. He made a circle in the air with one of his hands and pointed in front of him with the other. Then Brandon took off.

He had just told Joe he would circle the town looking for other Zombies, and Joe could take care of what was immediately in front of him. Joe loosed his other sword and followed the closest screams. He had work to do.

He had tracked the other members of Derek's crew and killed them where they stood or knelt on a victim. He had slashed through their necks, severing their heads.

Joe returned to the front of the diner and looked around. Brandon was nowhere to be found. It wasn't like Brandon to not follow his own orders. Joe wasn't worried about him, but something just was right. He couldn't put his finger on it, but whatever it was made him feel sorta funny, sort of uneasy.

Joe took off to the edge of town to see if he could locate his friend. He had motioned he would start in the west and work counterclockwise heading to the north, so that's what Joe did. He retraced what he hoped had been Brandon's path. If Brandon had gotten into a pickle, this was the surest way to find him.

Joe walked a few short minutes toward the north. The town was relatively small so it wouldn't take long to find his friend. He walked slowly so that he could be as thorough as possible. He only had to make a couple of detours to look down alleys that weren't straight.

He came to the north end of town without seeing his friend. He looked around, then looked toward Brandon's house. It was a small three room building with a covered front porch. The front door stood open.

Joe's brow furrowed as he walked toward the house. That uneasy feeling he'd had earlier returned in force, so Joe walked faster. As he approached the house, he saw that the door had been forced open. The part of the frame where the door lock should have been was gone. The uneasiness in his gut flipped inside out.

Joe walked in the door, knocking as he entered. "Brandon? Hello?" He thought he heard something coming from the dining room. He readied his swords and walked toward the sound. What he found stopped him in his tracks.

There on the floor was one Derek's boys, now headless. On

the floor near the headless corpse sat Brandon holding his wife. He held Jelena's lifeless body in his arms as if cradling a child. Her arms and face had bite marks where she had been gnawed on like a piece of raw steak. Blood still ran from the wounds. Tears flowed down Brandon's face, wiping away dirt from his sweaty face as they fell to land on his dead wife. His mouth was closed, yet an almost silent moan came from his chest. It was as if his very heart cried from the loss.

Joe said nothing. He went to the living room, sat down and laid his swords across his lap, at the ready. He would stay with his friend as long as he needed while he grieved his young wife's death. He knew what was coming, and it would be worse for Brandon than her death. Death can be mourned. But what do you do when death becomes something else?

And so, Joe waited.

Author Bio

The stories that I create are dark in nature. Foolhardiness is now mixed with that love of the grotesque and the terrible which has made my career a series of quests for strange horrors in literature and in life. I live in the shadows of the land between dark and light. Without light, there is no darkness, and without you I can't be me.

https://stefanlear.com

Spaceship Earth by Michael Gillett

"Mommy, how long did the first people live?"

"The very first people? People that could think? Perhaps, if you believe the records, less than a hundred years."

"Sad..."

"Not so very much. They lived under the stars. They lived a full life, for what they knew."

"I wish I'd seen the stars. Real stars."

"And me as well, sweetness." The child's mother sighed, "Me as well."

The young one looked back into the vast empty caverns behind them, down the newest fissure running kilometres into the empty distance.

"Was our life full?"

"Yes, darling."

Another quake shook them. A small quake. The two ignored it.

"Did your mother see the stars?"

"My mother?" The woman thought hard a moment. It was long ago. Over nineteen hundred years. My mother and father had chosen to leave, she remembered. They'd won the choice.

With the resources left to them, up until a few thousand years ago, there were perhaps two star-ships that could be launched yearly, each with a capacity of ten thousand souls. Generation ships, designed over a million years ago and launched every few years since. Many were aimed into empty space, to find their own way. Most targeted the known stars holding the uncertain promise of a future. A journey that only promised to get them off the surface of their hell-world. If the ships held-up, then they would still be en-route today, carrying the hopes of humanity.

She glanced upwards to the vast cavern's ceiling arching a hundred kilometres over their heads - their stone-grey sky with an artificial sun that warmed their world. Dust rained down through the red air as the ground continued to vibrate.

The Earth continued to tear itself apart. She'd vowed this would not be the last thing she saw. They would see their star before they died.

Would her own dear mother still be alive? Maybe...

The last woman felt her daughter's hand in hers and she looked down, the child's eyes a blue as bright as the sky of legend once was.

"Yes," she answered her daughter's question. "My mother saw the stars. They left on one of the last ships. She was a lucky one."

"Are we lucky?"

The woman looked to her daughter.

"We are very lucky."

Not as lucky, perhaps, as the many that made it off planet. The generation ships... a curse? To live and die in an iron coffin - yet under the stars.

But they had a chance.

Those remaining either made the best of their lives or ended themselves as they saw fit. A five-thousand year lifespan was a different sort of curse for those not having the strength to accept death at their own hands. The woman felt her daughter warm hand, and thanked her God.

She had been blessed. Never cursed.

"We made it to the end," the woman finished.

"How old am I?" the child asked as if not hearing.

"You are eleven. Still a babe. My little babe."

The ground shook again, this time violently and she felt her daughter squeeze her fingers.

"When will we die, mommy?"

The woman squeezed back, and replied, "Soon, sweetness."

"That's good then," the child replied. "Can you tell me again about Hans and Aelio?"

"Of course," the woman replied, and turning away the viewer and its images of the molten surface of the Earth, she started.

"Many, many millions of years ago, so the story goes-"

The blast of the rail guns blowing their cargos of deep stone over the horizon was shadowed by the flash and concussion of the latest attack. A very large detonation this time, and Hans looked back through the thick clouds of dust that had settled at the breach in the cliff wall. It had to happen, sooner or later. The battle had raged though this morning's bloody sunrise, no less fierce than when the first waves of Wattenfolk raced the real gun launch complex two weeks ago. And now, after the dust from the chemical explosion had cleared, he could see the entrance gate to the Great Hall exposed.

Hans felt a shiver course his body.

He was an engineer, not a fighter. The oceanic peoples had

no compulsions against killing his people - even as his own brothers died to prevent killing their attackers. Death was not the answer, and the fight was most illogical - though he understood their fear of the terraforming project. Most all his people were strong of mind and weak of flesh and it was yet another miracle that they'd held the Wattenfolk off for as long as they had. Not that miracles were a thing anyone put faith in. Technology was the answer, had always been the answer, and remained their one and only hope for a future.

If their fighters breached the barriers this time and passed on their learning to the rest of the Wattenfolk across the oceans, in their ignorance, extinction would be guaranteed.

The rail guns roared again, as they'd roared every hour, every day for tens of thousands of years, and as the sun crested the horizon the angry red disk over an arm's breadth in span provided a vivid reminder of what was at stake. A distant reminder, yes - much further than the immediate problem - but ultimately the only problem that mattered.

The excavation of Spaceship Earth was almost finished.

A bolt of energy from the Wattenfolk positions arched over-head and rained down lightning on the scorched and burnt earth - the sun scorched Earth. The smell of ozone was heavy. Hans made his way back to the entrance to cavern twelve, his home and work place. The tunnel that had been buried under the rock until now lay exposed and vulnerable.

He leaned hidden and protected beneath an outcrop then crouched deeper under his energy shield as arcs of blue light-ning flickered and stabbed at anything grounded. It would be difficult to defend the gates as long as they rained lightning. Hans had no desire to leave the protective bubble of his shield, but the Wattenfolk female that he'd watched crawling through

84

the shallow crevices towards him was carrying the stolen null generator on her back - and if she got by him, which she would not, that could indeed be the end of his dream – and how he dreamed of an end to this insane war.

She was intent on her path and hadn't seen him. Hans pulled back into the side of the cliff wall where the tunnel to the Great Hall had been laid open. He timed his entrance back into the caverns with the shutting off of his shield and prepared to assault the woman by hand. He'd not risk an exchange of null energy, but the risk of hand-to-hand was certainly just as fatal. He'd have one chance at landing a single blow to take her alive. If she made it past him and deeper into the complex she would be killed by the gate defences.

He crouched in the darkened alcove as she past him at a dead run, pulling at the pack on her back, apparently believing her target was close at hand. She looked just as human as he was, her being Wattenfolk and an oceanic creature. Her shield protected her and filtered breathable air, but did not block his view of her face.

She as not as ugly as all of that.

He let her get a few moments ahead, deep into the great hall so that there could be no help from any of her compatriots that may slip in behind and deep enough that there would be no easy retreat. Hans listened to her crashing footfalls far ahead and counted ten before setting off after her, his own run silenced by his null boots. He caught her after only a few moments, tackling her much heavier body to the ground so violently she'd not even had time to grunt. Hans doubled over in agony, feeling like he'd just broken his back. He'd been careful where he hit her, though. He needed the woman alive.

85

Engineering associates Veran and Chalk stood shoulder to shoulder between him and her, their arms crossed in defiance. Hans felt helpless that after all of this, these two could ruin everything.

"She's Wattenfolk."

"Do I look stupid?" Hans replied with a sniff to staunch the bleeding from his nose.

"You acted stupidly. Irrationally."

"You've recovered the Null Generator," Hans nodded to their captive. "I only want her."

"Your plan - your stupid plan - was not sanctioned," Veran reminded him.

"And your plan? The Councils plan?"

"We will prevail," Chalk relied.

Hans pointed to the Null Generator lying on the bench, its power packs removed and destroyed. Next to the evidence sat the Wattenfolk woman in a chair bound by field wire. She not spoken a word yet, but glared at them with intelligent eyes that glistened.

"When the next wave, or the next, or the next finally break through-"

"They have never broken through," Veran said to the woman with a look of disgust and pity.

"Not in seventeen thousand years has a single Wattenfolk made it this far," Chalk added.

"*She* made it this far," Hans said, also to the woman.

"Yet no further," Chalk finished.

"And you're all willing to allow this fight to continue another thousand years. Or ten thousand?"

"It's their doing -"

"It is your doing!" the Wattenfolk woman hissed.

86

"The argument has been made, and yes – our doing," Chalk replied. "The Wattenfolk have chosen in their ignorance to believe the end of days is a falsehood."

Veran laughed at that, and even Hans had to keep himself composed.

"The Wattenfolk race is of the ocean and you and yours would see us exterminated."

"How she talks!" Veran exclaimed in a triumphant giggle that was cut off by the sudden lurch of the earth below their feet and the deep bass booming of another quake.

"You see what you accomplish," she muttered. "You are afraid of it as much as we."

The floor shook again, this time side to side, and the two engineers grabbed at each other and the bench to remain standing. Vern knelt to the floor and spread himself over the bare rock floor. The quake subsided even as he was grasping for a finger hold in the polished stone, and with a look of catlike embarrassment leapt back to his feet, the suspensors woven into the soles of his boots providing the illusion that he had the strength of the ancient ones.

"Go ahead and have your talk with this... creature," Chalk said as he and Vern quickly scanned the readings on the sensors they wore on their wrists. "That quake was not one of ours. We've dug deep enough to set the seals. We have real work to do," and at that the two of them turned back down the Great Hall, all but gliding across the polished floor in their null boots and were immediately far out of site.

Hans turned to the woman and realized he was still squatting and holding the floor like a frightened child and he quickly stood as well. She looked up at him.

"Your weapon is destroyed," he said.

"Do I now look stupid?" She replied with a feral grin.

"You look... intelligent."

"You can count on that," she replied with a tome that hinted of further resistance.

"I am definitely counting on that. More than you could ever dream."

Hans adjusted the bonds on the chair, turning them off, and the woman fell forward helplessly. Hans leapt forward to catch her before she could hit the floor, the impact of her body knocking into his giving rise to a yelp of pain.

"Are you that weak?" she grunted as she climbed to her feet.

"You know it." Hans looked at the ruined generator and then back to the woman. "So. How clever are you?"

"More than you know, apparently, but perhaps not enough," she smiled ruefully. "I am no longer interested in the dying part of the contract– though I suspect I could still hurt you."

"Not enough to matter. We both know that. We both want to live."

She had an attractive smile. Attractive for a Wattenfolk woman, Hans supposed. No... He changed his mind. There was a relaxed smile on her face, and her eyes had a light to them that twinkled. She was indeed attractive, he warranted.

"Our two peoples have been fighting for a very long time."

"A way of life. To preserve our way of life."

"And in all these millennium, you had no interest to find out more."

'None at all. You exist most unpleasantly underground, while we live free in the oceans. We are not suited to each other, neither intellectually nor spiritually."

Emotionally though... Hans felt an irrational hope stirring in him. And why not?

"Can we talk?" he asked.

"Will you lie to me?"

Hans laughed at the archaic notion.

"Lie?" as asked. "If I understand the word, then you believe I would mislead you by distorting or manufacturing certain facts?"

The woman's eyes narrowed and her forehead furrowed and she nodded, "Yes. Lie."

"There is no benefit in distorting the facts. We put our faith in the facts. We eat and digest facts. My people do not lie. It would be a sacrilege."

"Sacrilege?" the Wattenfolk woman snorted. "What Gods would you offend? The same ones that watch you rip this Earth apart?"

Hans paused, then looked up at the cavern ceiling far over-head.

"You've seen the sun. Bloated and red. It was not always so. It is dying. One day it will rip this Earth apart far more efficiently than I could, believe me."

"Believe you?" The Wattenfolk woman repeated, a look of puzzlement on her face. "I'd like to. This conflict drains us. We have no evidence that makes you trust worthy. Ocean levels have fallen to dangerous levels. We live a simple existence, with no need for the-" and she paused to gaze at the null boots he wore, "...devices that seem to fascinate your kind so. We have faith in our own ways. We do not use engines to swim."

"We are different, I grant you that. But not so different as that. We live on the same planet, just different environments. We once all lived on the surface - a very long time ago. We adapted. Come down with me, let me show you our home. This place you believe to be the cause of your people's destruction. Perhaps see it first, as it really is? Let your instincts guide you then."

The Wattenfolk woman stood and stared. Her eyes watered and she took a breath and let it out with a sigh.

"Aside from the fact, as you call it, that I don't have much choice, I agree. Show me what you will."

"Thank you!" Hans replied, his heart pounding unreasonably hard. This was a historic moment, even if the council didn't see it that way.

He touched the pad on his wrist and the woman scowled curiously.

"I summoned a cart."

"We will ride? You are so weak you cannot walk?" she laughed at him.

"I can walk. I doubt you could. I think you misjudged. The generators are far from here. I suspect you could never have found them, if you survived long enough to look."

"Thanks for the respect," she smiled again, her teeth so white it almost hurt to look a them.

"You're quite welcome. My name is Hans," and he held his hand out to help her out.

She took his hand and stood beside him. "My name is Aelio."

Hans smiled again, feeling something unfamiliarly warm in his chest.

"Hello, friend Aelio. Pleased to meet you, I think."

The council met the two of them in an emergency session. They were, of course, in an uproar over Hans and his uninvited guest, but considering she was captive they acquiesced and gave him permission to try and tame the wild woman. Perhaps an element of fear over how she'd made it so close to their home had finally softened their heads enough to try another attempt at negotiations.

It took several days of exploring before the cart dropped them at cavern twelve's control room. The 'flight deck', the techs there called it. En-route there'd been many stops, too many wondrous sites for Aelio to comprehend and she'd became overwhelmed. They visited briefly hospitals and crèches. The compact cities that went deeper than she could grasp. Curiously sweet air, skies of stone so far above that she could only trust it was so. Hans was even permitted to show his guest one of the hundreds of rail gun launchers.

"Why such a violent mechanism?" she'd asked.

The trigger man pointed to the trainloads of stone waiting export. "We couldn't use everything for building materials. With unlimited energy available to us, this is the most efficient way to be rid of it."

She stood aghast as each carload was deposited in turn into a chamber an launched via acceleration tubes many kilometres long.

But now, they were here, and the great map of the Earth was about them and Aelio was overcome again.

"My Gods, this place is vast."

"We are not, as you may have thought, worms crawling through tunnels. We've built the environment capsules for Spaceship Earth."

She swept her arms through the projection, across the oceans her kind had settled and touched at the caverns to where the surface people were fleeing. "My people are taught stories of those that remained below the surface. The underground people - they laughed at your ways. My people live in disdain of your ideas and reject them."

"How can you, then. Still..."

"How can I reject what I now see with my own eyes? I cannot. We have been stupidly ignorant."

"Why the fight, for so long?"

"We are a different in every way. We had nothing to share. When we felt ourselves under attack, it was as if an alien race were systematically destroying us."

"And perhaps we were..."

"Of course you were. Did you have no idea what the consequences of draining the oceans would be? Do you have a plan?"

"I'll be honest. I have a plan, but it is mine own. The counsel would hear nothing of it."

"What plan?"

"To capture one of you. To show you the evidence. To convince you that our solution is the only solution. To stop the war. To save humanity for a while longer."

"For how long have your people been digging?"

"A very, very long time. The fusion reactors have been running forever, powering the guns that remove the rock as we dig - and provide the inner-global heat and air conditioning and pretty much everything else."

"Unlimited energy - the gunner indicated that."

"Almost. Not enough to save us, but enough to give our children and our children's children time. You never know."

"Save us from what?" she asked.

"The sun. The Earth will fall into the sun. There is no way to stop that. We've tried many times to explain to your people, but they could not accept it. Let me show you."

Hans brought up views of the solar system - a simulation of the sun and planets, and Aelio watched as the sun's core started its slow collapse and the ejection of it's atmosphere. He paused the projection.

"Aelio - watch now. I move the Earth maybe a half million miles further away from the sun and see?"

The sun shrunk and the earth slid further out in it's orbit and at maximum solar atmosphere expansion, the Earth was still outside the danger zone.

"You see, our very best understanding and projections show that we could have survived the expansion if the Earth had a more distant orbit." Then the screen reset, and the sun's atmosphere caught up to the retreating Earth, catching it. The Earth, caught in the very tenuous atmosphere, slowed its orbital speed and fell onto the sun where it was consumed.

Aelio watched with eyes wide, and Hans assumed the reaction she showed was one of fear.

"As you can see, the Earth dies. This is an ironic fact. The Earth in a safer orbit would most likely never have evolved life. To date, mankind has discovered what there was to discover. There is no magic. Life is fragile. In our universe, even stars die. But we humans chose not to die so quickly. We had to start, and we did. Today we still work to prepare Spaceship Earth to survive the times ahead. There will be an exodus. The technology for faster than light interstellar travel does not exist, and the generation ships being built are ready - see here."

"You'll launch from underground?"

"Yes - in the time to come there will be nothing on the surface. No air, no water. Nothing. There will be oceans of molten crust. But we'll launch the ships until there is nothing left to launch with. We must survive as log as we can."

"I see."

"Your people will die if you stay where you are."

"Perhaps."

"But if you help us..."

93

"We are water folk. We are farmers."

"You can stop the war, help us to move the oceans underneath and in a way that every one of you can be saved along with us. In time, we will become one people again. We will remain human."

Aelio's gills flapped open a moment, and Hans eyes widened in surprise as she took his hand and pressed it against her neck and he felt her heart beat.

"We can breathe the air, still."

Hans felt her warm hands on his own neck. Her fingers probed with curiosity his flesh for a moment, and then she dropped her hands to her side. "Same heavy heart beat. Same warm-blooded heat." She sighed. "But we live free in the Oceans. We are... compared to all of this, perhaps, a little bit wild..."

"Live in the oceans to come - live with us. Show us how we can become better. Help us. Help yourselves."

And then he felt her hand in his.

"You'd let me go?"

"This will be our children's home for untold generations." Hans looked at Aelio, at her large lidded eyes, tiny ears, gill flaps, her long legs and strong arms. His chest ached. "Could be our children's home, one day," he repeated, hoping she'd heard him.

"Or we could simply die," she murmured to herself.

"Have faith," Hans whispered. "We have faith. You and I will surly die. But the human race will not simply fade away and vanish."

And for a very long while, Hans and Aelio simply stood together, holding hands, the first of their kind watching together the projections and dreaming impossible dreams.

And then he let her go.

###

"And did they live happily ever after, mommy?"

"Yes and no. The story goes that it took many hundreds of years to convince both sides that there was a way to save themselves. Perhaps even thousands. The people lived long lives even then. The children of Hans and Aelio saw the start of unification and the beginning of the new humanity."

"I love that story," the young child sighed.

"It is the last great story we honour. It gave us all this time."

"Did your mommy live a long time?"

"Yes – and my grandmother and her Grandmother. We all lived a very long time."

"Did your mommy love her husband the way you loved my daddy?

"Eventually, yes. Love no longer comes easily, but when we choose to love, it becomes real."

"Do you miss my daddy?"

"Not as much as that - he died before you were born, when the walls collapsed. He died well. I'm happy for him."

"Why did you want to stay when so many others chose to end themselves?"

The woman looked at the image of the sun through the viewers. It was a maelstrom that filled the entire sky while oceans of molten rock writhed and leapt as the Earth shook itself apart.

"I wanted to see it happen," she said as another great fissure opened silently behind them - and then the stone sky cracked open and the red sun poured in.

The child squeezed her mother's hand.

"Me too," she said.

Author Bio

As an IT professional for over 35 years, Michael does his best to find time to write, read and participate in the writer's life. He's currently president of IFWA and has been a member for more than fifteen years. He enjoys writing urban fantasy, a bit of hard SF on occasion, a bit of historical fantasy on occasion and really enjoys humor when he can. He has a short story published with Absolute Express (imprint of Edge Press) which was nominated for an Aurora award for 2011, and is working hard to become a published novelist.

Current Publishing Credits:

Enigma Front (Contributor)

The Picnic by Ellen A. Easton

Tommy smiled, his thoughts far away from the food on his plate. Just two more rotations and then he had a full thirty six hours off duty. He'd put in so much overtime lately, he started to feel like one of the factory drones.

His long time friend Erica had persuaded her project lead to give her some time off-site to research, and replenish the lab's stock of raw materials. Tommy had convinced her to book the same time off as his and tomorrow evening they were heading out. The old forests on the west side of Star Haven would be perfect, both for the abundant materials as well as the peace and quiet. Tommy was overdue for a change of scenery and time away from the pounding rumble of the factories.

He quickly finished the rest of his dinner, and walking over to the sanitation station, pressed a series of buttons on the attached screen to clean up the plates. Back in his quarters, he scanned all the schematics for the area, downloading the maps into his memory for easier access the next day.

"If only everything in life could be learned by download," he thought laying down on his sparse cot. A quick half hour rejuvenation sleep, and he would be back at the factory. "I have to remember to check on the cooling vents in tube five," Tommy thought, drifting off. "They've definitely been sluggish lately."

Erica sighed, watching as the green haze slowly dissipated inside the test tube. She picked up a nearby beaker, carefully tipped in a few granules of a pale yellow powder, and then leaned back in her chair, waiting for a reaction. Nervously biting her lip as a new, dark green fog danced about the test tube, she entered the results into the console beside her. Standing up, she turned and took stock of the lab. She certainly needed to replenish her supply of Vetrium 6, along with some of the soil samples. The mechanics had been nagging her about producing a better cooling agent for days. She needed some time off to clear her head and find inspiration.

Slumping back into the chair, she sighed and reached for another beaker.

The Western Plains glowed with a soft pink light as dawn crept over the hills beyond. Tommy and Erica lounged comfortably in the speeder, invigorated by the crisp outdoor air. Grinning, Tommy pointed out a nearby field on the console display and turned the speeder as Erica nodded enthusiastically. He dropped the vehicle gently on a level spot and hopped out, plucking the box that held their breakfast from the rear compartment.

"You've packed us quite a spread," Tommy said as he pulled out colorful containers of all shapes and sizes. Placing a large blanket across the damp grass, he started to organize the food. "We might not even need lunch after this."

Erica smiled at the compliment, then pulled a mineral reader from her pocket and scanned the nearby boulders, picking out the compositions in the varying internal sediment layers. She compared the analysis to the lab supply list.

"And you picked a great spot, Tommy," she said, settling on the blanket and grabbing a plate. "I can get all the samples I need from this area."

Half an hour later, surrounded by empty plates, Erica leaned back on her elbows, bathing her face in the sunlight as she listened to Tommy pouring coffee. Sitting up, she graciously accepted a cup, then smiled as he proffered up his own for a toast.

"Here's to the best chemist the lab could have hoped for." He glanced sidelong at Erica and grinned, running a hand through his unruly hair. "You'll blow them away with another brilliant solution as usual," he said, bringing the drink to his lips. Returning the grin, Erica started to raise the cup to her lips, then paused and frowned, staring intently at the ground. Pressing her free hand firmly against the dirt at the edge of the blanket, she felt the ground shiver and then saw small pebbles and rock chips vibrate.

"Tommy, can you feel that?" she asked in a worried voice as the stones grew more exuberant in their movements. She put down the cup and slowly stood up, trying to place the source of the vibration. Tommy ran back to the speeder, grabbed a pair of binoculars and began scanning the horizon.

"The tech logs didn't mention any unusual activity in the forecast for today," Tommy stated with a frown. "This definitely isn't natural." He dropped his arms to his sides and turned to look at Erica. "I think we'll have to head back early." He didn't wait for a response and started packing up the remnants of their breakfast.

Erica watched the ground shake and reverberate, her frown mirroring that of her companion.

"Tommy, if this isn't natural, then it must be coming from some heavy duty tech. And the only machinery even close to this area is . . . home." She gasped, the color slowly draining from her face and ran to grab Tommy's binoculars. Scrambling up onto the top of a stone outcropping, she stared in horror at a large plume of black smoke crawling its way slowly up into the sky. The bottoms of the clouds took on a hollow mockery of dawn, reflecting the fires below.

"I don't think we can head back," she whispered in a quivering voice. She lowered the binoculars and slid down the outcropping. "Take a look," she said. Tommy stared at the plume that continued to rise, separating into multiple tendrils that wove in a sinuous dance across the horizon. They appeared to beckon to him. As the smoky tendrils caressed the clouds, he turned slowly to face Erica with a sick look on his face.

"I knew I was forgetting something when I left this morning," he said, his face turning a pale green. "Do you remember when I told you how the cooling vents were acting up, and I was on duty to repair them?" Erica nodded slowly. "Well, I was so distracted by our trip, that I completely forgot about them. And now..." He flinched, running a hand through his hair. "You always get me in so much trouble," he told Erica, watching her out of the corner of his eye.

The way he was looking at her made the hair on the back of her neck stand on end. She drew in a breath to retort, when a blinding flash of light consumed the horizon, chased by a deafening roar that flattened the trees and slammed her into a nearby boulder. Shakily standing, she put a hand to her mouth and winced as she felt the deep cut on her lip. Cracking her jaw to try and clear the ringing out of her ears, she found Tommy stumbling several feet away, trying to get his bearings. Grabbing a survival kit from the speeder, she pulled his arm and shouted.

"Head for the rocks! We have to get underground in case there's another explosion."

Tommy stared at her blankly. The ringing in his ears sounded like deep whispers. He shook himself like a wet dog, focused his mind and accessed the program for natural formations. He scanned the area with fresh understanding.

"This way," he pointed at a broad, shallow crevice about fifty yards away. "There's a fissure leading to an underground tunnel. We just have to make an opening. Stand back," he warned as he pulled a gun out of their emergency kit. "Some splinters might ricochet this way." Shielding her eyes, Erica watched him blast the rock apart to reveal a small chasm hidden inside the cliff. Coughing, Tommy grabbed Erica's arm and they ran inside. Turning on a flashlight, he used its beam to guide them further inside the chasm, looking for a spot to rest and catch their breath.

After several minutes, the tunnel opened into a large cave, where small crystal stalagmites covered the ground, twinkling as they reflected the flashlight beam. The effect was disorienting and Erica steadied herself on a nearby rock face as her vision spun with the lights.

"Erica, go through the pack and see what supplies we have. I'll take a look around and see if there's a safe way out of here," Tommy said, placing the gun on the ground and looking around. Erica nodded and dug a pack of matches and a small candle out of the kit. She lit the candle and began to sort through their remaining supplies.

Tommy rounded the corner, losing sight of Erica. He tried to focus his eyes for another scan of the rock structure, until he heard a soft scratching sound from further down the tunnel. Tightening his grip on the flashlight, he quietly edged down the passage, trying to shake the whispering voices from his mind. As he rounded the corner, the tunnel opened into another small chasm.

A small pool of water glistened on the far side, with occasional, arrhythmic ripples teasing his mind that inhabitants resided below the surface. Large stalactites hung from the ceiling, dripping what looked like ichor, but upon further inspection appeared to be some sort of decaying mold. Cautiously, he explored a bit further, then paused and cocked his head. The deep whisper was growing louder, then suddenly it was no longer a whisper. It was a hissing wail. Tommy dropped to his knees, holding his hands to his ears trying to block out the sibilant voice. He blinked, looking up at a pair of luminescent eyes watching him from the other end of the pool as the voice continued. After several minutes he slowly stood up, ran his hand through his hair and nodded.

"As you wish." Turning, he returned to the chasm where Erica was applying a salve to her broken lip.

"That was fast," Erica said softly, closing the lid on the salve. "Did you find anything?" she asked hopefully, standing up and brushing dirt from her pants.

"I did," he replied, kicking over the candle and walking towards her. He grabbed the gun and shot. The sharp bang echoed through the cavern followed by an endless crashing of rocks as the bullet shattered the wall behind Erica. She stared in dismay as rubble filled the exit.

"Tommy, what are you doing?" Erica cried out. "We're

trapped!"

"I know." He knelt casually and drew a small but wickedly sharp sampling knife from the pack.

The last thing she saw as he stepped toward her before the candle flickered out was his smile.

The Picnic by Carl Bolton @guerillaillustrator on Instagram

Author Bio

Ellen A Easton is an avid reader and long time gaming and fantasy buff. She is currently published in four anthologies and is working on her first novel. She lives in Cochrane, Alberta with her fellow gamer and writer husband, daughter and several black cats.

Find her work on Amazon at amazon.com/author/ellenaeaston

The Cataclysm by L. Douglas Hogan

THE CATACLYSM

On July 3, 2027, Wormwood reached our little blue planet. Before the meteor's arrival, it was believed that we were alone in the universe. The cataclysm that followed would prove the sceptics wrong. The world wasn't saved by the biggest military or by the greatest economy, it was saved by the intellect of one of the greatest minds of our time. A high school kid with no ability to hear or to speak. His name was Wayde "Odie" Odom. All he left for us was a journal. It was enough.

Wayde Odom's journal was found on the streets of Farmington, Missouri. It is preserved here, in Chester's Public Library, for the world to see.

Date: August 19, 2032

"I lost everything. EVERYTHING! I'm writing this journal under duress. I understand that I might not live another moment. Every breath I take could very well be my last. I got lucky, finding this blank journal to keep for posterity's sake. It's old and very dusty. It was laying next to, what I can only assume to be, the bones of a little girl who must've died shortly after the Clysm. It's crazy. For the past several weeks, my only company has been the bones of the deceased. I don't think I've seen a living human being in three months. Maybe more. It's hard to tell what time of day it is – you know, with the sun being darkened out and all.

"Before I get too far ahead of myself, maybe it'd be appropriate if I introduce the author of this journal. My name's Wayde Odom. My friends used to call me *Odie*, probably to make light of my good attitude. I was fortunate to have grown up in a home with a mom and dad that took the time to learn sign language. Yeah, I'm deaf and I'm also a mute. That means I can't speak. I don't know why. I've been told there's a science behind it, but I really haven't taken the time to learn it. There was a time I might have, but the Clysm changed everything. Since I lost my journal, I guess I should explain everything like you're reading for the first time. I can only assume that when the course of the world's events have come to a dire end, there will be nobody alive to tell the story. When that happens, there'll be nothing left of history, except the artifacts we leave behind.

"The Clysm began five years ago, in the year 2027. I remember like it was yesterday. When you can't hear, the things you see tend to stick to the back of your brain a little while longer. On that particular day, I was going to graduate high school. Graduation was cancelled. There I was, sitting at the kitchen table with Mom and Dad. Normally, they'd be getting ready for work, but they were still in their PJ's. We were watching CNN and the news headlined something like, METEOR TO IMPACT EARTH. Having a 4.0 average in high school, I was fairly knowledgeable to the fact that our planet is hit by meteors constantly, but this was different, and the

"Countdown to Impact" sub-header proved it. My parents said they'd been watching it all night. Apparently, the government, scientists, and an array of astronomers had been monitoring the meteor for weeks but didn't want to alarm the public. So, they kept it quiet. Allegedly, they didn't know if it was going to be an Extinction Level Event, or E.L.E. as it was also called. Well, it was.

"I stayed at home that day and watched the countdown with my parents. They were memorable moments that will always stick with me. We rehashed memories from my childhood and even a few from before I was born. The meteor hit the earth, somewhere in New Jersey, at 1:17 P.M. Eastern Time. There were a few reporters crazy enough to stand at ground zero when the meteor impacted. They were brazen reporters and I must give credit where credit is due. Their recordings went black at the moment of impact. I remember CNN went from white noise to the International Space Station. I'll never forget that eerie camera angle. There was a cloud that erupted from the impact site and slowly spready across the eastern United States. It slowly dissipated somewhere around Ohio and Kentucky. We were thankful and we counted our lucky stars.

"I never graduated. School never resumed because of the loss of life just from the impact of that meteor. Those from the immediate area, that sought shelter and survived the impact, died soon after. At first, there was fear, panic, and paranoia as reports of paranormal deaths began to circulate. Nobody seemed to understand what was happening on the east coast. We'd never find out either. The paranormal deaths began to spread. One by one, we lost news station after news station – newspaper after newspaper. Eventually, zero news was coming from the east coast.

"I'll never forget my next memory. A reporter from Chicago was sent to ascertain the events and mysterious disappearances and deaths on the east coast. We were tuning into a broadcast from a local FOX station when the reporter began his broadcast. He started recording from the western tip of the point of the last known report of paranormal activity. They parked their van and exited the vehicle. The cameras were rolling. He mentioned his name and what he was reporting. He had armed security with him. As he was talking, there were screams, then the sounds of gunshots. Lots and lots of sounds of gunshots. The cameraman pointed his gun into the direction of the screams and gunshots. The entire event was recorded live. It looked like there might have been a few seconds delay, because the screams stopped, the gunshots stopped, and then the station went to white noise before it reverted back to the local anchor on FOX.

"Over the next few days, it was more of the same. The paranormal activity continued to spread north, south, east, and west. Eventually, it reached Illinois.

"I remember every detail from the morning my parents died. I woke up, just like any other morning, and headed for the television. They were calling the meteor 'Wormwood.' Religious zealots of all sorts were evangelizing the television set and preaching their respective brand of Christianity. That's when we started praying. We weren't particularly religious people, but we believed in God. We prayed. When we were done, we prayed some more. I prayed in my mind, since I couldn't speak. I figured, *the Lord knows my heart*. I sat there, with my eyes closed. I went through my usual prayer and what-nots. When I opened my eyes, there was blood everywhere. I looked about and my parents, or what was left of my parents, were scattered about the kitchen. My mom's head, spine, and a portion of her left arm were in the corner. Her innards were nowhere to be seen. Her legs and her other arm were in the front room. My dad was similar, except I found parts of him in the bathroom and in the backroom. I tried to scream, but you know how that went.

"I grabbed Dad's cellphone and dialed 911, but that was a useless gesture. To this day, I don't know if they received my call. Even if they did, they didn't hear much. I left the house and found that mine was not the only family to fall victim to the violence, whatever it was. People were dead in the street, at least what I assume to be people. The Unseen, as they would later be called, had shredded the people to little bits, violently strewing their parts across the neighborhood. I was panicked and had no clue what to do. I couldn't call for help, but even if I could, who would answer? I saw no living human for several hours.

"Later that day, I saw a girl, about thirteen years old. She was hiding under a table in a restaurant. Body parts blanketed every inch of the room. She had her mouth covered with her hands. That's when it dawned on me. *Sound.* I extended my hand to her, but she refused to take it. I left her alone and went about my business.

"Fast forward four and a half years. That's when I met Rebecca (the thirteen-year-old, who just turned eighteen). She remembered me, but she didn't know a lick of sign language. She wrote everything out to me on a piece of paper. Needless to say, I carried a lot of paper. By this time, I had a backpack full of journals and pencils. I carried very little that wasn't recorded history. A biography, of sorts. Rebecca told me that the day I had found her under the table, she thought I was one of them because I wasn't dead like the others. She had to learn on her own how to survive. She hadn't spoken this whole time, for fear of *the death*. 'The Death' is what she penciled on our writing tablet. She said it's what the radio used to call the killing of people by the Unseen.

"Living with the Unseen for so long allowed us to learn a great deal about what was happening. True, we didn't know what they were, but we suspected they came with Wormwood. What we did know was that they were invisible creatures, possibly living between planes of existence, that could harm us, but we couldn't harm them. Somehow, someway, they were able to cause damage to our plane of existence, but we couldn't faze theirs. This gave them the advantage. At this point, we had no idea what their weaknesses were, or if they even had any. From what we learned of them, guns had no power over them. Just racking the bolt of a rifle, or pulling the slide back on a pistol, brought with it certain death – a very violent death. We learned to survive by hiding. It seemed that I had the upper hand in this arena. In the old world, I couldn't speak, and I couldn't hear. It's still true, but now they are not weaknesses. They are strengths. What lesson have I learned from this? That weaknesses are fluid. I cannot speak and that has saved my life multiple times. I can't hear, and so I don't react negatively when the Unseen attack in my presence. I simply close my eyes, and in the few moments it takes for the Unseen to do their thing, I open them, and I am a lone survivor.

"Last week, Rebecca and I were scouting for food. We entered this old farmhouse and found the owners' bones scattered about the property. We tried to avoid the canned goods. It was just too risky to open them. Rebecca shared with me that cutting metal is noisy. Boxed goods that could be quietly cooked seemed to yield the best results. The Unseen didn't seem to be affected by the firelight. Neither daylight, heat, nor fire seemed to draw their attention. It was only sound. Water stopped flowing from the faucets a long time ago. And electricity? That's gone, too. We're living just like they did in the days of the wild west, except we don't fear bandits and gunslingers. No, we have something way worse. Anyway, Rebecca found a box of pasta and sauce, but to cook it, we'd need to bring some water to a boil. I only had a little bit in my backpack, and she didn't seem to have any at all. Luckily, we saw a pond in the back yard. An actual waterhole. We walked together through the sloping valley that lead to the fishpond. That's when everything changed. Rebecca had a boiling pot in her hand. She used it to scoop up some water. I was standing next to her as she stood up and suddenly froze as she was walking away. The hairs on the back of my neck stood on end. I knew something terrible was happening. I was at a loss because I couldn't hear what she was hearing. I was frozen in place, as well. Not because I was hearing something, but because I was following Rebecca's lead. The more I studied her, the more I realized she wasn't hearing anything at all. She was seeing something. She was staring deeply into the pan of water and she couldn't take her eyes off of it for a moment. Whatever it was, it had her full attention. I slowly walked up behind her and glared down into the water pan. At first, I didn't see anything. But after switching my position, there it was. I can't explain what I was seeing. It was the them, the Unseen. They seemed to be phasing in and out of our spectrum of sight. I looked up to see if I could see it, but it was only visible through the reflection of the water. It wasn't constant, either. Colorless, almost shapeless. It's hard to explain on paper and even if I had words...I'm unsure if I could tell it. TTFN"

What did you learn today? I stare at Rebecca when she's not looking. I think I like her.

What fun things did you do today? Nothing. Surviving isn't fun.

How did you make the world a better place today? I floundered.

Date: September 7, 2032

"Dear God, why did you take her from me? Why is this happening? I know I didn't grow up religious. It's not my fault, is it? Did I do something wrong? Why was I spared? Why? Rebecca was the best thing to happen to me. I was loving someone for the first time. Am I not supposed to love? Am I not supposed to be happy in this hell on earth?"

What did you learn today? That love is pointless. After more than a year of living with Rebecca, I learned that nothing in life is a guarantee. Nothing!

What fun things did you do today? There's no fun in death.

How did you make the world a better place today? I held a silent memorial for Rebecca. I picked flowers and left them where she was ripped from my world.

Date: September 10

"It was the second saddest day of my life. The first being the death of my mom and dad. This time my eyes were open. I saw the whole thing. I saw them rip her to pieces and all I could do was watch.

"It's been a month since we discovered we could see them in the reflection of the water. We never went anywhere without a water pan. We tried mirrors. That didn't work. It has to be water. The more I think about it, the more I begin to recall the lessons of biology and science from my last two years of school. Water is the natural medium of all cells. This has something to do with why we can see them through it. It looks like rain is headed in this afternoon. Instead of taking shelter, I'm going to go out, boldly, and test my hypothesis. If I'm right, I should see them without a looking glass of water. TTFN"

What did you learn today? It's more of a memory than a lesson. I remembered that water is essential to all life. It's a natural medium to all cells. If I can use that to my advantage, somehow, I might find a way to hurt them.

What fun things did you do today? Nothing.

How did you make the world a better place today? I watched a colony of ants as they rebuilt their castles. I gently blew the soil away and they rebuilt it. What did I do? I kept them busy and gave them purpose. God, I hope I have a purpose.

Date: September 11

"It worked! The rain is my looking my glass. They're everywhere. They phase in and out of our plane as if they're trapped between realms or dimensions or whatever.

"I used this opportunity and took full advantage of my newfound knowledge. I threw rocks, sticks, metallic debris, everything I could think to use at the beings. Everything passed straight through them like they weren't even there. They didn't even respond until the object hit the ground and made a sound.

"I've had a revelation. As I sat here thinking about mediums and particles, wavelengths came to mind. I think I might know of a way to cause damage to the Unseen. It's a long-shot, but if I'm thinking correctly about all this craziness, it would mean that I could use a spectrum of light to inflict damage to them. It makes sense in my head. Water is a conduit for virtually all life, apparently even beyond the Earth. So, if I can find a way to shoot an electromagnetic wavelength less than 400 nanometers at the Unseen, it should cause the protons in their body to light up and actually cause some damage. TTFN"

What did you learn today? Rain works kind of like a costume on them. It surrounds their bodies and gives me their outline. I still can't see any real detail, but I can see they're there.

What fun things did you do today? Fun is for children. No fun.

How did you make the world a better place today? I'm still working on that.

Date: September 12

"I spent what was left of yesterday and all of today walking. I had this great idea, but the nearest laser is nearly forty miles away. I'm thinking Office Max, in Farmington, Missouri. I covered a lot of ground and seen a lot of carnage along the way. I took the highways from Chester to Farmington. Every vehicle I saw, along the way, had a different story to tell. All of them had their drivers ripped from existence while the cars and trucks were still in motion. Each vehicle in Drive. Each driver and their passengers, dead. Not even a broken window. It's like they phased through the cars, killed their prey, and phased out. The Unseen have never eaten their prey. It's like they're hungry enough to kill, but the hunger dies with the victim. It's the weirdest thing.

"I brought my tarp shelter, though I'm hesitant to use it. There's a call for rain tonight and I worry that the sounds of the rain hitting the tarp will draw the predators in on me. If they come, I'll never know it, because I'll be asleep. TTFN"

What did you learn today? I had an epiphany. I'm thinking I can affect the protons in their body. I mean, why not? Protons are shared across planes of existence. It makes sense in my head.

What fun things did you do today?

How did you make the world a better place today? (see

previous day)

Date: September 13

"They came. The rain rolled in and with it, the thunder. The biology of the Unseen is radically different than ours. Their bodies lit up like Christmas trees when the storm's energy hit. I was awake most of the night watching mother nature pick them off one-by-one. They seem to draw lightning, but never survive the strikes. This gives me hope that my idea might just work.

"I finally made it to Office Max. I found the laser pointers that I was looking for and loaded them up with batteries. I couldn't find anything that produced less than 400 nm, though. The lowest wavelength available to the public seems to be 405 nm. I'll try it. Hopefully the next rain will be soon, and I can put this to the test. TTFN"

What did you learn today? I learned that the Unseen can definitely be killed. I watched them vaporize with each lighting strike. It was like the Fourth of July and Christmas all rolled into one.

What fun things did you do today? I watched them die. It was amazing fun.

How did you make the world a better place today? I went to Office Max and hijacked a laser pointer. I stole it for posterity's sake.

Date: October 4, 2032

"It hasn't rained in three weeks. For the first few days after the storms, I used the water-filled ditches and potholes of water to navigate around the Unseen. I learned something new. You can walk straight through them if you do it quietly. They can't be felt, and they can't feel you unless there's sound. That leads me to believe that they somehow operate using kinetic waves. I'm not sure how, because it makes sense that they would take damage from kinetic projectiles like bullets, if I'm right. Literally anything kinetic should cause them damage. There's still a lot to figure out. I'm just living a day at a time and learning as I go. Eventually it will come to me.

"Finally! It's looking like rain. I've chosen to stay close to Office Max, just in case. I found a farm home just out of city limits where I can hide and wait. I am still weary about the city. Not only are the Unseen a threat, but new threats have arisen. People. People have grown increasingly more dangerous. They're learning how to survive against the Plane Jumpers. That's what I'm calling them now. I guess I can get away with calling them whatever I want. Who's going to stop me? Anyway, people are ball-gagging themselves to keep from using their mouths. I see them from time to time though my binoculars. I keep my distance. Eventually, they slip up. Usually when they're foraging for food. Some clumsy person will bump a shelf or drop an item. Their deaths are not in vain. Each time, I learn something new. For example, I saw one kick a can. It rolled down the aisle of the store, and the longer it rolled, the longer the Plane Jumper could see its prey. It's like the kinetic energy of the can sent sound waves throughout the store, bouncing off the aisles and walls, much like the way a bat's echo-locator works, except the Plane Jumpers weren't providing the sounds, the humans were. The Plane Jumpers simply responded to them like they suddenly had eyesight. They kill everyone that moves within the area of the sound's influence. There was another instance where a lady bumped a shelf and it drew the attention of a Plane Jumper, but once it was at the exact location of the sound, the kinetic vibrations had stopped, and the predator had lost its prey. It's for this reason I have wrapped my soft-soled shoes in fabric. Now, they make even less noise than they would normally have made. At least that's my guess, being deaf and all.

"It's raining outside and I can visibly see the Plane Jumpers. They just stand there in one spot. I choose not to get too close to them because I know that I can hit them with this beam of light from a great distance. But I want to get close enough to them to see what they look like. Up until this point, I have not had a good look at them.

"They're translucent. I can see through them, but only enough to cause the objects on the other side of them to be displaced, sort of like looking through a thick piece of glass. I only occasionally see arms and legs. Multiple arms and legs. It's hard to tell how many because they are restless creatures that seem to move about in one spot. They never stop moving in place. Almost like they're trapped until freed by kinetic energy. I'm going to try a little experiment before I tag them with this laser. I have no idea what will happen when I do, so for the sake of science, I want to try a few other things.

"Okay, so I found an old swing set and moved into position. I grabbed the seat of one of the swings and slowly pulled it back. I was hoping it would be squeaky and it was. I released the seat and remained very still. The rain was falling softly at this time. As log as the swing squeaked, the Plane Jumpers were able to move. Once it stopped, they locked in place. I remember that heavy rains fill the air with quite a bit of kinetic energy, so I assume the best course of action would be to shoot them with the laser while they're trapped in the slow rain, because once it picks up, they will see my movements.

"It worked! When I tagged one of them with the laser, they all responded. It looked like the Plane Jumper was screaming, only I couldn't hear it. The others seemed to hear it, though. There are dark clouds moving in. I'm going to head to the loft of the barn and remain still until the storm passes. Maybe I'll watch the lightning pick them off again. I admit, I'm a little discouraged that the laser didn't affect the creature a little more than it did. It only wounded it. Overall, I'm happy with the results. We have a way to kill them. If only I had something more powerful. TTFN"

What did you learn today? That the Plane Jumpers rely on kinetic energy to see. They see through soundwaves. Vibrations, to be precise. Anything that can make a kinetic vibration can attract them.

What fun things did you do today? I caused pain to one of them. It was trapped and I took advantage of it. The low wavelength in the light spectrum of a laser pointer causes them damage. The lower the wavelength, the greater the pain.

How did you make the world a better place today? I discovered a means to kill them.

Date: October 5

"It's been raining for two days. I'm out of food. The ground looks clear. I saw a big one earlier. It was moving about the property, but I haven't seen it in a while now. I have to risk getting out of this barn and go in search of something to eat. I know that once I start walking in the rain, I will be visible to them and they will be visible to me. I only pray that I see them first. God, if you're out there, please keep me safe. Let my life be worth something meaningful. You've spared me until now. I'm confident there's a reason behind it.

What did you learn today?

What fun things did you do today?

How did you make the world a better place today?

It is believed that Wayde never made it to his destination. Those who have analyzed the writings of his journal believe that he would not have dropped it and left it behind. The dark stains you see on the bottom of each journal page are believed to be Wayde's blood. It's impossible to tell, since we don't have any DNA to compare it too. He mentioned the bones of a girl, the journal's original owner, but the DNA consists of one X chromosome and one Y chromosome. These markers are exclusive to the male gender.

Because of Wayde Odom's experiments, survivors of the Clysm managed to build weapons capable of killing the Plane Jumpers. Although we still know nothing about their origins, we now know they can be killed.

Author Bio

L. Douglas Hogan is a U.S.M.C. veteran with over twenty years in public service. Among these are three years as an anti-tank infantryman, one year as a Marine Corps Marksmanship Instructor, ten years as a part-time police officer, and twenty years working in state government doing security work and supervision. He has been married over twenty-five years, has two children, and is faithful to his church, where he resides in southern Illinois.

Find his books on Amazon at amazon.com/author/ldou-glashogan
His Facebook page is L. Douglas Hogan, Author
His Instagram instagram.com/LDouglasHogan

His website url is www.LDouglasHogan.com

Sign up for his newsletter at http://www.ldouglashogan.com/
newsletter.html

Wasteland Wanderer by T.D. Ricketts

His leather rode up and piled up just above his waist. He pulled it down again, cinching the waist belt tight. *Lost another inch in the waist*, he figured. He stopped on the military crest of the hill looking out over the rolling prairie. It looked flat as a pancake but there were undulations and hollows all over that could hide the undead. He had been walking forever. The years since the pandemic swept through the world had been rough, but now the undead were just falling apart. It reached a point where they couldn't move, ligaments and tendons falling apart. They had nothing living to feed on and the bacteria or virus or whatever it was that kept them moving could no longer sustain them. At least, that was his best guess.

He had grown up with the life-and-death struggle. Running and hiding. Watching everything and everyone he knew die, as the dead never quit.

The wind whistled and moaned across the open land. Ahead was what looked like a small village and one huge oak tree. He slowly walked towards it, more out of curiosity than need. His pack had smoked meat and some greens he had picked along the way. Thinking about food made his stomach growl. Stopping again to survey what he saw, he pulled some grain from a pocket. Some wheat he had found in his travels had somehow managed to reproduce and germinate. It was amazing. He crunched the seeds as he stood there looking. English ivy covered several buildings. No telling what they had been before. He slowly made his way down the hill. Stopping and looking and listening. It took a while to get there but slow was safe, and safe was fast.

The ivy blocked the entrance of the first building. He slowly peeled it back. The interior was dark and smelled like death, feces, and rot all rolled into a big ball of crap. As he set foot over the threshold, the boards gave way, cracking and falling into the basement. Moans filled the air as the boards hit the floor. He backed up cautiously and left. It wasn't worth the danger to check that one out. The best thing he could do was torch it and burn whatever lived in or was trapped in the basement. But first, he wanted to look around the other buildings.

The next building was block construction. Chunks of mortar fell out of the gaps between some of the blocks, but it looked surprisingly intact. The door was laying on the ground in front of the building, the glass smashed and long ago buried in the thick mat of grasses growing there. The windows were just empty eyes staring out at the world. They watched the world move on without them. The smell of this building wasn't as bad as the other. Just moldy and damp. The roof had collapsed flat but still shielded the interior from the worst of the weather. Just inside the door, he saw something on the floor. The metal body of some small toy. Not sure what it was, he picked it up and turned it over again and again. It looked like some kind of carriage without the horses. He had seen horses once. They had either been eaten by the dead or by the living.

He shifted his bow to his off hand and shoved the toy into his pouch. Maybe someday he would find someone to trade with and there was no telling what it could be worth. Besides, it was kind of neat. He looked out the windows and realized that night was falling. Looking around, he saw the oak tree. That would work. The large oak had many limbs, and several were large enough to sleep on for the night. Pushing his long grey hair back, he tightened the band holding it. It was just a strip of cloth, but it was old. Smooth and shiny black, so soft and light. Not like the homespun clothing he wore, patched and repaired with whatever skins were at hand.

He quickly climbed up the tree. A thick limb parallel to the ground was his bed for the night. He unstrung his bow and placed it into his quiver, placed his pouch on the top of the limb, then tied them both down so they wouldn't fall. He stretched out on the limb, wrapping a blanket around himself and tying himself to the limb, quickly falling asleep. Once, during the night, a snuffling and snorting sound woke him. It sounded like some sort of hog or something. No need to worry as it probably couldn't climb a tree.

Looking over the limb at the ground below, daylight was just breaking, and the dew was heavy on his blanket with a deep chill to the air. He slowly untied his tethers and reclaimed his quiver and bow. He quickly checked the bow for dampness and water damage. All was good, so he climbed down the tree and stood facing the remaining buildings. There was nothing different from last night, so he moved to check out the other buildings.

The first one was a collapsed mess. Ivy covered it and the roof had collapsed into the building, sending the walls outward. No use wasting time on a death trap. Even if he could get into the building, he couldn't see to look around. Odds of finding anything useful were getting worse and worse as the years went by. Most places had already been stripped of anything useful. Trying to grow food was a beacon for the dead. If you stayed too long in one place, they found you, and they never quit until you were dead.

The last building looked to be in decent shape, "decent" being a relative term. Moving towards the door that was no longer there, he paused. Listening for the moan of the dead and hearing nothing, he picked up a rock and threw it into the building where it clattered across the floor. Still listening, he heard nothing. Not even the sound of birds making any noise. He remembered what they looked like and the sounds they made. It had been so long since he had heard one sing its good morning song.

The boards creaked as he stepped on them, but they held his weight. The living room came first but there was nothing useful. A molding pile of wood and fabric was all that remained of a couch and a chair. A few rusty bits stuck out but they would fall apart the minute he touched them. He had tried that before. The windows were broken and gaped wide open. There were no curtains. Once, he had found enough material to make a dress for a girl who was now long gone. His shoulder ached and there was a soreness in his hands that never seemed to stop bothered him. He shook his head and turned back to the house. He hadn't seen another person in years.

He moved cautiously into the kitchen. Cabinets stood with doors hanging, their empty insides exposed to the world. A rusty hunk of metal lay in a corner. He had no idea what it was for, or what it used to do.

So far, it had been a waste of time. This house had been stripped may times over. Just a crumbling waste. A remnant of days long gone and people that used to be. It made him sad to think that they may have had a life and loved ones that were yanked away. But that wouldn't help him survive now.

The first floor yielded nothing, so now it was time to get on with the scary part, the basement. It seemed like there was always a corner or a nook and cranny that something had been stuffed into to hide it. He remembered years ago when he had found a jar with some kind of preserves in it. The concoction was so sweet, thick and syrupy. He had eaten a spoonful a day for a month and licked the jar clean.

He found the steps that lead down. They looked to be solid from above. He stepped down on the top step. It creaked and groaned a bit as he eased down onto it. He relaxed a bit and took another step. Slowly he made his way down the steps, and then it happened. The steps didn't give way. His left leg went all the way through as the board beneath it fell. The riser that held them in place broke and as his weight came down on the next step, it split. The long narrow jagged piece of wood jammed into his leg. It pierced the bottom of his calf through the muscle, exited through the top of the muscle, then stuck into the back of his thigh.

His left leg dangling, and his right was impaled on a broken step. The pain was excruciating. Even the tiniest movement sent waves of searing pain through his leg.

And then he heard it, just a small scrape. He went wild trying to lift his body out of the predicament it was in, but the scrape became louder and a slight moaning filled the air like a gentle summer breeze. He was trapped, and something was below him. He couldn't see what was there, lurking beneath him. The blood from his wound started to drip down the piece of wood. The patter of the blood hitting the floor sounded loud. This was an arterial bleed. He felt hands grab his leg. He kicked and screamed. The hands wrapped around his ankle like a vise. No matter how much he shook his leg, they wouldn't let go. Weight pulled down on his leg stretching it downward. This drove the large splinter of wood deeper into his thigh. The pain was excruciating.

He realized this was probably it, the end of his life. He would end up as one of them. One of the living dead, doomed to live his life trapped in this house moaning and yearning for the flesh of the living.

When the steps collapsed, he knew the end was at hand. His body crashed down onto the hard cement floor. Pieces of wood scattering all around him. He reached forward, looking for anything that he could use to fight. His quiver was within reach and he pulled his broken bow from it. His heart dropped when he saw the two pieces. The halves were still stout wood, tapered to a point, kind of like a wooden sword.

His leg screamed in agony as he moved but his options were to either lay still and die or fight and die. The source of the moan was standing there looking straight ahead and facing away from him. If he made no sound, it wouldn't find him. He laid there and thought. He had to think his way out of this mess. It meant getting close, and that went against his policies. Keeping away, running, and hiding had kept him alive for a long time. If he could stand up, he had a chance to stab one half of his bow into its eye. Destroy the brain and destroy the zombie.

He leaned forward and sat up. The wood in his leg scraped the floor and he let out a moan of pain, a muffled groan that made the thing's head snap around. There was no time to waste so he lurched to his feet. Keeping his weight on his good leg and leaning forward, he thrust half of the bow forward at the dark shape that was closing the gap between them. He felt the wood make contact and hope surged within him.

Teeth clicked as it stumbled forward reaching for him. He realized that the bow missed the eye, just tearing a gouge along the side of the thing's head. It was turned to the side by the blow to its head, but it still reached a bony, parchment covered hand for him. The hand swung wide and caught the back of his head, drawing him forward. The broken, jagged teeth reached for the flesh that it craved. It wouldn't stop and wouldn't be denied. Its desiccated form came closer and closer. Pain shot through his body as the jagged teeth bit into his skin.

He couldn't feel his body. The form hovering over him moved away as his body jerked and twitched. His control over his body seemed to just disappear. He let out a moan as all reasonable thought fled from his mind and was replaced by a hunger for flesh that doomed him to wander the wastelands.

Author Bio

T.D. Ricketts is a resident of the mighty mitten. Aka Michigan. An avid hunter and fisherman, spending time outdoors helps make him happy. Addicted to short stories and working on several books at the same time. He has been in many award winning anthologies and to date has had over 30 short stories publish. You can find him on Amazon and Facebook. Stop by and say hi as he loves chatting with people.

Find his work on Amazon at https://www.amazon.com/T.-D.-Ricketts/e/B075WKS2HY

The Pit by William Stuart

"When I was a child, my aunt and uncle had a farm. My parents would take my sister and me on weekends to play with our cousins while the adults drank beer and talked about grownup things. Sometimes, we'd spend the night or the weekend camping with our cousins, Davy and Holly.

Davy and Holly had real camping tents and sleeping bags and we loved to set them up when we went over. Uncle Victor would build us a little fire and we would roast marshmallows and tell ghost stories until bedtime. One of the adults would eventually call, "Lights out!" from the porch and then we'd turn off our flashlights and try to sleep. On some nights it was warm and clear enough that we didn't even need tents. My aunt Sarah would bring a bunch of blankets and pillows out and we'd have a giant pallet where my sister and cousins and I would just lay there staring up at the stars.

I used to love those trips, laying on my back on my little lumpy pad, face and fingers sticky with melted marshmallow, just staring into the sky. On some nights, one of the adults would come sit with us and point out constellations or planets, or even

129

satellites if they could spot one. The stars were so beautiful and there were so many! Staring into forever, watching the smoke rise into the cosmos, I wondered so many things like, 'Is there a God? Is he watching me right now? What does he do all day? Does he like marshmallows too?'

I know, it's not profound, but I was still amazed. Awestruck. Humbled, and filled with wonder at the limitlessness of space and time. I wanted to touch it. I wanted to breathe it. I wanted to swim in it.

I wrote little poems and songs about the stars, about the night sky, about Orion and Cassiopeia. I read everything I could— I read mythology, I learned the constellations, I dreamed of being an astronaut and sailing across the cosmos, of shaking hands with the infinite...

So, that's me. what's your story?"

There was silence as I stared out across the pit, watching plumes of smoke drift into the canopy high above. There had been less of it, the smoke, in the last two or three weeks. In times past, that might have been taken as a hopeful sign, an indication that things might be getting better. But time and experience had shown me that a little slow-down merely meant you needed to gather the coals to make the pit burn hotter- to consume as much material within as possible. Because it wouldn't be long before we were going to need the room.

Realizing I wasn't going to get an answer, I stood and straightened my dress before taking up my stick and beckoning the girl to follow me on my rounds. She moved without a word and we set about the grim task of stoking the flames. Large piles of seasoned timbers had been stacked every few hundred feet around the hole, with smaller piles placed at intervals between them. Trucks arrived daily to replenish the stacks, regardless of whether we needed it. In slow times, the piles would grow so large that it was hard to imagine that so much fuel could ever be burnt. In busy times however, we often ran out. And when that happened, it was bad.

Out of the pit rose a dozen crane towers equipped with swivel arms and clamp claws. The base of each tower was sheathed in a protective cylinder of concrete a dozen feet thick all around to protect the already specially-treated steel from the tremendous heat of the fires. The concrete shafts came up to ground level; the cranes another fifty feet above them. Each of the cranes had a control box that allowed us to pick up a load of fuel, then position and drop it where the fire was burning low. We could also use the claw to move material around inside the pit to ensure an even, white-hot burn. Our goal was to make sure that anything that went into the pit was reduced to ashes quickly and that the pit itself remained unfilled for as long as possible.

The girl stood next to me as I grabbed the controls of the crane. I showed her how simple it was to operate the claw.

"They wanted to make sure that even a child could work it, so there's no special technique. You pull this to release the safety, then just go like this." I turned the wheel to the right and the arm spun on its swivel until the claw hovered above one of the wood piles. "Then you push forward like this." The claw opened and dropped into the stack, "And then pull back," The claw closed on the wood with a crunch and then retracted to the end of the arm. "Now turn left and it goes back over the pit and then hit the trigger to drop." The claw opened and dropped the stack into a dark part of the fire. Almost immediately, the load burst into flame and our sooty faces were lit by the bonfire that raged fifty yards away. We watched it burn until the pile collapsed on itself and faded from white to yellow to orange, about ten minutes in all. Finally, I locked the crane into position and grabbed my stick. "Let's get cleaned up and find something to eat."

The canteen was large and well-lit, having been built to accommodate dozens of round-the-clock workers and their families. The barracks next to it was merely a high-rise apartment complex that had been named thus because it was a military installation. But the names were the only 'military' thing about them. No expense had been spared to ensure the residents of this compound were comfortable and happy, as much as that could be accomplished given the circumstances.

We went to the walk-in cooler and chose our supper from one of the seemingly endless stacks of boxed meals. My companion picked turkey and stuffing while I settled on chicken pot pie. It wasn't the most healthful or appetizing repast, even from what was stored in that cooler, but we were both tired and preferred a four to six-minute turnaround time to what would be involved should we break into the good stuff. It wasn't something to worry about. There were only two of us and enough food to feed a small village for months. We could afford to be lazy.

We peeled the plastic sheets from the trays and placed our meals into two of the dozen microwaves and waited. I glanced at the girl. She was young, maybe early twenties. From her clothing and hair style I could tell that until very recently she'd enjoyed a life of privilege. Or whatever passed for privilege anymore. I almost felt sorry for her, but sympathy was somewhat difficult to conjure now. And all it did was make me sad anyway, so I didn't try too hard. The ovens dinged, and we carried our steaming trays to one of the long benches that stretched across the cafeteria.

"So, as I was saying before, I wanted to be an astronaut and

132

was working toward that, but wouldn't you know it, astronauts have to be really good at math and I never was. I struggled with basic algebra, in fact. And with the way everything turned out, I'm really glad I didn't work too hard trying to learn either!" I laughed, trying to lend a little levity to the room. The girl's haunted countenance didn't respond, not even a little. "Tough crowd," I said finally, before digging into my dinner.

We ate in silence for a while. The girl looked thoughtful a handful of times as she poked at her mashed potatoes. I kept waiting for her to say something, but she never did. After a time, I let impatience get the best of me and I snapped.

"Listen. I know. Okay? I know. Everyone you love, right? Everything you knew? Yeah. Me too, toots. Me too. But you know what? We don't have time for this shit. Okay? Any minute, that bell is going to ring, and you and I are going to have to deal with whatever comes because we are, at the moment, the only ones here to do the job. Okay? So, ditch the silent treatment, and do it now. You don't have to be interested in my astronaut stories but you sure as hell better start responding when I say things. Got it?"

The girl just stared at me some more. Her expression hadn't changed. She just looked stupid and sad and now a little scared. She lowered her head and said nothing. No breakthrough. Great. I stood up, grabbed my stick, and said, "Whatever," before heading out of the cafeteria toward my apartment. I saw in the reflection of the giant plate glass windows that the girl was putting our trash in the bin and then following behind me. I was about to turn and tell her to piss off when the alarms sounded.

Lights flashed, and sirens screamed all across the complex. In every room an automated message played repeatedly.

Attention! Attention! Cargo inbound! Repeat, cargo inbound!

Transport arriving at gate E-C in five minutes. Please proceed to your stations immediately. Hazmat suits must be worn by all personnel at all times when cargo and cargo transports are present on the property.

The girl ran to my side and looked at the speaker that issued the message.

"Well, you heard the man," I said, "Let's get to work." I turned back the way we had come and walked across the cafeteria again, spinning my stick casually. The girl was at my side once more and we walked together down the hall. When I reached an exit door, she grabbed my arm.

"Wait," she said.

I stopped. "Yes?"

"Hazmat suits?"

I looked at her and for a very brief moment, I really did feel sorry for her. She was not made for this world. Hers had been a life of stuffed animals and pink things and brunch. It wasn't her fault any more than it was mine. The world just didn't care. I just couldn't for the life of me figure out how she'd made it this long.

"Don't need 'em."

"Don't need..."

"Useless."

"But, the alarm, the message..."

"Recorded before the guys in hazmat suits figured it out."

"So, they just... stopped using them?"

I narrowed my eyes. Was she serious? I just sighed. "Yep. They took too long to put on and take off and then wash and they weren't any help, so they changed protocol."

"But the message?"

"Remember, this is a *government* facility. The change order for the announcement is probably sitting on some bureaucrat's desk somewhere waiting for an approval. I wouldn't hold my breath." And with that, I walked out the door toward east gate C.

"What is it we, uh, that you do here?" The girl asked when she caught up.

"Didn't they tell you when your ticket got punched?"

"No. I, uh..."

"Weird. Okay, well, you know how it was before? When you would take your cans up to the street and the guys with the trucks would pick it up and take it away?"

"I remember taking out the trash, yes."

"Well, they took it to a place, right? This place is sort of like that."

The girl thought about it for a few seconds as we walked at a brisk pace toward the other side of the compound. When we reached E-C, we stopped and waited. "You remember what I showed you about the crane and the claw?"

She nodded. Then, "You mean this is where they send the dead? Rather than burying them?"

"Something like that."

"We... We just burn them?"

"As quickly and as thoroughly as possible."

"But..." She just stared for a moment and then fell silent. She nodded and hung her head as she walked to the opposite crane control. Any minute now and we'd see how much this poor creature could actually handle.

The alarm sounded again and spinning red and yellow lights flashed atop the gates. A few seconds later there was a hiss and a hum as the large steel doors swung inward and a semi-truck backed slowly into the compound. It continued its slow roll until the wheels were aligned with the guidelines painted on the asphalt. A second later, the large clamping mechanisms that kept the shipping container attached to the trailer opened automatically and then the platform it sat upon tilted, dumping the container on its end. The truck sat idling while I prepared to do my part. I looked across at the girl again and shook my head.

Piloting my crane, I guided the claw to the box. A hook in the throat of the claw caught on a loop on the top of the container and I lifted it up and out over the edge of the pit. I pointed at a yellow spot in the coals and motioned for the girl to use her crane to dump fuel there to make a white-hot, intense flame. When she was done, and the fuel was well consumed, I was ready. I looked over at the girl and saw that she was watching the container, waiting to see what was going to happen next. I sighed at the simplicity of innocence. I swung the box over the fire and then hit the lever.

All at once the bottom of the container popped open and two hundred men, women, and children fell screaming into the flames. It was fast. As mercifully fast as I could make it. Most were immolated immediately by the intense heat. Some, however, burned for a few seconds before their screams finally ceased. I waited a moment, then returned the container to the truck. I set it on the trailer and it aligned itself automatically. The clamping mechanisms closed once more, and the truck drove out of the gate. Within a few minutes the gates were closed, the alarms had been silenced, and it was only me and the girl who now stood trembling in front of me, every horror she'd ever dreamed dwarfed by what she'd just witnessed.

"Pretty rough, huh?"

She said nothing.

"Come on inside. I need a drink."

We crossed back to the canteen and I helped myself to two bottles of Captain Morgan from the nearly endless liquor supply in the larder. I handed one to the girl, then unscrewed the cap from mine and took a big gulp. "Drink up, sis. There's plenty and it will go to waste if we don't drink it. And I don't want your cooties."

She took the bottle from me but her expression told me she wasn't ready for jokes just then.

"Okay, okay. Here's the deal. When you got your ticket punched, what happened?"

"I, uh. I was walking with a couple of friends and my monitor just started beeping. Like, I wasn't even testing. It just went off on its own.

"Um, then a couple minutes later a drone shuttle showed up and the app told me I had to get in. Nobody ever said anything. The shuttle didn't even have a driver. It just brought me here. Oh my god! You just burned all those people!" She said, finally crying.

"Yeah, about that. I asked you when you got here but you never said anything before now. How is it out there? I haven't gotten any outside news in a long time."

"It's, uh, normal? I guess. More normal that it's been in a while. The monitors and the app are working, finally, and so people are going back outside. There's lots of commercials for the app and the monitor and they want to make sure everyone has it on and it's charged and that they're testing three times a day. But it... like, it works, I think. It's helping get infected out before they get sick."

"Getting them the help they need?"

"That's what the commercials say."

I shook my head and laughed before taking another swig. Fuck it, I was going to get drunk tonight. It wasn't like if another cargo came in, I'd mess it up and hurt someone somehow.

"Oh, Mary, Mary, Mary. Poor, sweet Mary..."

"Excuse me?"

"Ever hear of Typhoid Mary?"

"I think, maybe?"

"Back before there was proper sanitation and vaccines, typhoid was a bad deal. Typhoid Mary was a cook who worked for a bunch of families when the disease was an epidemic. She infected people around her, but never got sick herself."

"I don't understand."

"You know what, Mary? You never told me your name."

"It's Jenny."

"Jenny, when you go to bed tonight, you need to thank god and the heavens above that you got picked up by that shuttle instead of getting sent to a *CuraClinic*. Do you understand what I'm saying?"

She thought about it. She was a bit slow, but it finally registered. "Because the *CuraClinics*... They just send everyone here?"

"Bingo. Now, when I first got here there were still some people around working the place. Official people. We had three or four cargo an hour coming in for days on end. Trucks were backed up for hours. It was really bad. But, back then the trucks had a mechanism that would release a gas so that at least it was painless, like going to sleep. I don't know if the infected were dead or just sedated, but they weren't awake when the boxes opened.

At some point they either they ran out of gas or they ran out of people to fill the tanks or, I don't know, something, because

THE PIT BY WILLIAM STUART

cargo started coming in live. Nobody on the outside would tell us anything, so we just dealt with it. Now all cargo is live. Anyway, one by one the folks here succumbed and went into the fire."

"They just... All those poor people go in for help and the ones who are supposed to help them just shove them in a truck and throw them in the fire?"

"Oh, I'm pretty sure they walk onto the truck on their own. But, yeah. They think they're being taken to a hospital for treatment. But there is no treatment. Once you've got it, you're a goner. And if you start showing symptoms, you're far more infectious to those around you. So, they get you gone as fast as possible."

Jenny took a little nip from her bottle, grimaced, then followed it up with a slug. "And you?"

"I'm what you call an asymptomatic carrier. Like Mary. I have it. I'm positive. But I never developed symptoms. At first, they thought maybe I had some genetic marker or natural immunity or something. So, they brought me in for tests. But no luck. At some point, I'll get the fever and I'll have to go into the pit with the rest. I'm guessing that's why you're here too. You're like me so the extra time you have will be best served dumping the infected. Or, Hell, I don't know. Maybe you weren't infected, and they just started tapping randos to help out since everyone else is dead," I shrugged, "Your guess is as good as mine."

She clutched her bottle tight enough that her knuckles were white. I didn't blame her; it was definitely a hard pill to swallow. I took another slug off the booze and really felt the warmth well up inside me. Was it just the booze or had I finally gotten the fever? I couldn't know and had long since stopped worrying about it. My time would come sooner or later, best not to dwell on it. We sat quietly and sipped rum a while longer before the alarms sounded again. I grabbed my stick and my bottle and headed outside. Jenny carried her bottle too as she walked beside rather than behind me for the first time since she'd arrived that morning.

"Marine biologist," she said, finally, "I wanted to study whales…"

Author Bio

William Stuart lives in Texas with his wife, two daughters, and a grumpy old dog. When he's not writing scary stories, you can find him taking on way too many projects and hobbies at a time, reading comics, magazines, or books about monsters, or sweating in the garage trying to figure out how to bring dead things to life.

Find his work on Amazon at https://www.amazon.com/William-Stuart/e/B07HHK2X5F/

Satan's Apocalypse by Kevin J. Kennedy

When everything ended, I was just a kid. I wouldn't say I was too young to understand, though. Once day life was normal, and then everyone started acting crazy. We couldn't go out of the house anymore. Just Dad would go, but he went for food one day and never came back, leaving only me and Mum. We still needed food and Mum wasn't up for leaving me on my own, so she had to take me with her. We would go on food runs together and gather what we could, then head back home.

Food became sparser and although there were less people around, the small numbers that had survived had done so by becoming more brutal. People had started just taking what they wanted, and they would do it by whatever force they found necessary.

Eventually we had to leave our home as there wasn't much food around and the gangs had started ransacking all the houses nearby. We moved around a lot, mostly at night. It was scary creeping through the streets in the dark, but Mum said we were less likely to be spotted. It seemed that after nightfall, everyone just partied and were too busy to be looking out for anyone, whereas through the day, they were all on the hunt.

That was a long time ago now. Mum has been dead for a while. I don't even know what happened to her. One night I went to sleep and when I woke up the next day, she was gone. I know someone must have taken her. She wouldn't have left me, but I don't know why they didn't take or kill me. Mum probably heard them coming and led them away from me. That was the type of person she was. Always looking out for her little boy. I wasn't that little anymore, though. I was fifteen when she disappeared, and I was strong for my age. Even though we didn't always have enough to eat, I would always train as hard as I could. I had strong genetics. My father had been a bear of a man and had been in the army for a large part of his life. I suppose that's where I got the whole 'keeping fit' thing from. That and the fact that I always knew that if I was strong, I would have had more chance of protecting my mother.

After she disappeared, I didn't really care about living any-more. So I started to take risks that I'd have never taken before. The first crazy risk I took was approaching a group of four guys that were sitting and having a drink around a bin that they had set on fire. I knew that if they all rushed me at once, they could have killed me, but I had stood and watched them for a while before approaching. I was confident that I could take each of them on their own and the fact that they seemed to be drunk boosted my confidence. They were a little older than me but not much. I just walked out from the trees and made a beeline towards them. I was almost on them when one guy jumped up and told me to stay back, quickly followed by his nearest companion, who drew a knife.

"Chill brother. I'm just looking for a heat. Can I join you?" I asked them.

"Who you with? You're too young to be traveling alone," the first guy replied. He was covered in dirt and smelled like shit.

"Aint with nobody. Travelled with my mum until she disappeared."

They looked me over and all four of them looked around, scanning the trees I had come from.

"Look guys, I'm on my own. Can I get a heat or what?"

After taking a few moments and whispering to each other, they obviously decided I was no threat.

"Fuck it. Take a seat little man," the smallest one said.

I moved in between two of them and put my hands next to the fire. It felt good to be warm but, on the inside, I was dead. My mother always taught me to be kind when I was younger, but as the world started to change, she taught me about the evil that people could carry inside. She still taught me to be a good man when possible and help others if I could, but I didn't see a whole lot of good growing up and when she disappeared, I decided that the last good in the world was gone.

The guys were pretty quiet. I think they were sizing me up. They spoke to each other and asked me some questions about my past. They passed a jug between them that contained some foul-smelling liquid but never offered me a drink. I just sat and stared at the fire. I could almost see my mother in the flames. There weren't many waking moments when I didn't think of her.

As time passed by, the guys got drunker. They were getting louder and, while they were trying to keep up a façade of being reasonably friendly, they were hitting me on the back and shoulders harder and smiling at each other. I'm not sure if they were just dumb or if they assumed I was, but it was clear they planned to hurt me. I knew that many people in modern times had turned to cannibalism, even if only on occasion, and I wondered if they had allowed me to join them, thinking that I would be their after drink take-away.

"Gotta take a piss," I told them.

I got up and walked about twenty steps away from the fire. I could hear them begin to whisper and it confirmed my suspicions. I stood for about twenty seconds and walked back to them.

"So, who's first?"

They all looked at each other. I could tell straight away that they weren't expecting it. I slipped my hunting knife from the back of my jeans and plunged it into the throat of the closest guy. His eyes went white. I'm not sure if in that moment he realised he was dead or if it was just the pain, but he was a goner. Pulling it out quickly, I lunged towards the second guy and stabbed him in the heart. My knife was sharpened every day. Sometimes several times a day. There wasn't a lot to do when you travelled alone, and it was a distraction from my thoughts. The knife withdrew from him relatively easily and I turned to the other two. The closest guy put his hands up in a show of surrender, so I slashed his palms open. The fourth guy took off running. Guy number three pulled his hands back as the blood started to gush. He didn't even try to make a run for it. I smiled at him as I moved closer and quickly slit his throat. I had no intention of torturing these people, but they were bad guys. I could tell, and the world was better off without them. I rummaged through their belongings and found that there wasn't much to take. I did, however, find a few torn pairs of girls' panties, which confirmed my suspicions that they weren't good people. Just as I had thought, good people have no place anymore. When the civilized world ended, it left only room for the animals. My mother was the last good person alive and I was sure as hell not going to go out like she did. I might have only been fifteen, but I was going to be the hunter.

After that night, I just kept travelling. I had heard rumours over the years of a bar that still functioned after the world ended. They were supposed to have beer on tap, and not the shit people brewed themselves. I knew it was probably bullshit. I had even heard they still had entertainment on each night, and it was like stepping back into the past. Even if it was a myth, I had nothing else to do with my time.

As I travelled, I wondered if I was part of the evil that walked the earth now. My mind went back on forth with it, but I concluded that everyone was either a predator or prey, and I had no intention of being the latter. It was rare that I came across other survivors but when I did, if they were a largeish group, I bypassed them. If there was four or less, I killed them. A few guys managed to pull their own knives on me, but the element of surprise always gave me an edge and I seemed to be faster than most people, even though my size was still growing.

A few months had passed when I arrived in the city that the mythical bar was supposed to be in. I had probably killed about twenty people by that point, all male. I didn't consider myself a murderer. I was sure that, given the chance, I would have been dinner for some of them or just a bit of entertainment for the others. I could see in some of their eyes the darkness that resided within. I never chased down those who ran away. But they were probably dead now, too. The new world was no place for the weak.

The city had been torn apart and set alight. There wasn't much left of it. I crisscrossed what would have once been the main section and upon finding nothing, I started to work my way further out. I told myself that if a bar had survived and was still functioning, it stood to reason that it was already run by psychos before things went bad.

Weeks passed by as I travelled. I only wished that there were still cars to travel in but not many of the roads were driveable anyway. I had almost given up hope and was going to start heading north again when I turned onto a street that was pretty well lit up. Not something you see often, or ever anymore, for that matter. I knew in that moment that I had found the bar. I crossed the road for a better look and, there, further down the street, was the bar. It looked like it had been untouched by the world around it. As I walked down the street towards it, I could see the neon lights above the door. It was called Satan's Apocalypse. I couldn't fucking believe it. The myth was real. A fully functioning bar with electricity and who knew what else.

I stood outside the door for a few minutes. I wondered what it would be like inside. I wasn't nervous. I knew that anyone who drank in here must be tough and probably scum but I was ready to die and was sure I'd take a few of the fuckers with me. I wasn't sure, however, that if I left and walked away that I would ever have another destination to go to. This was it. Something had drawn me here and I was a fucking predator.

I pushed the door open and walked inside. I stood just inside the door and looked around. It was a fair size and had neon lights everywhere. The place smelled of stale sweat, piss, and smoke. There was music playing from the juke box and a group of guys standing around the pool table. Mostly everyone looked over at me. I made eye contact with them all. After standing there for twenty to thirty seconds, I walked over to the bar. I had no money and doubted that they would deal in physical cash anyway.

I decided to stand at the bar rather than take a stool. I wanted to be ready for anything that came my way. The bar tender was a huge hulk of a man. Not all muscle though. One of those naturally big guys with an even bigger stomach. His head was clean shaven, but he had two little tufts of hair at the front, gelled into horn shapes.

"Help you boy?" he asked me.

"How do you get a beer in this place?"

"Need some tokens, kid."

I wasn't enjoying his 'boy' or 'kid' chat and I wasn't in the mood for riddles. I wanted to have my first beer at a bar before I would happily go to meet my mother, and that fat fuck was testing my patience.

"You going to make me guess how I get those or you gonna tell me before I start to get pissed off?"

He smiled wide. "I like that attitude, sonny boy. You might even have a chance of getting a beer if you keep that up. This bar is all about the entertainment. People come from all over and not many leave, if you know what I'm saying. You want a beer, take someone's tokens. Easy as that."

I turned my back on him and scanned the bar. I was confident that there were no good people in the bar. Certainly no one that I would feel guilty about hurting. Maybe the waitresses. They looked innocent. Maybe not innocent, but not evil. The rest, though, looked like they would rob their best friend. I didn't really care. I had come all this way and I wanted a beer. I didn't know if I would leave the bar, but I wanted to taste a beer before whatever was going to happen happened. The bar obviously traded in violence and I was no stranger to that.

Just as I was picking my unsuspecting victim, a tall skinny

guy who looked like a rat slapped one of the waitress's asses. She didn't do anything, but she didn't look impressed. I had my man. I contemplated for a minute or two if I should use my knife, then reasoned that I didn't need it. I was over to his side and he was too busy bragging to everyone at the table about what he was going to do to the waitress later. Little did he know, I had crossed the bar in seconds. I could still feel the bartender's eyes following me. I put my hand on my victim's forehead and pulled him backwards, pulling the chair with him. He had already been swinging on the chair and had no chance of catching his balance. When he clattered onto the floor, he looked up at me, eyes wide. He must have noticed I was a young lad and thought he would get the better of me as a smile spread across his rat-like face. He was wrong. My foot came down across the middle of his face and obliterated his nose. I could feel the crunch. I didn't stop. I must have stamped on his face eight or nine times and I could feel bone breaking each time my foot landed. No one at his table moved. Whether it was because I had taken them unaware, because they thought I was a psycho, or because they were so used to the violence and didn't really like Rat Boy anyway, I'm not sure. I knew he was dead before I stopped stomping him, but it was a good release. I could feel some of the anger I carried leaving my body. I bent down and searched his pockets. He had five of the tokens. I didn't know what they were worth, but I slipped them into my pockets. He also had a little metal baton. I took that too. I nodded to the men at the table and made my way back to the bar.

On reaching the bar, the bar man had a pint sitting for me already.

"That one is on the house, boy. That was quite a show you put on. I could see you fitting in around here. Be warned though.

Now you gave everyone a show, someone will likely challenge you."

I didn't even answer him. I just picked up my pint and took a swig. I had never tasted beer and I can't say I was all that fond of the taste, but I had earned it and I was going to drink it. As I sipped away, a bell rang.

"What's that for?" I asked the bar man.

"Shift change for the waitresses. They work twelve-hour shifts. We never close."

I turned towards the bar patrons and noticed that Rat Boy was gone. Somebody had clearly removed his body. The waitresses were all making their way out of a door and more were spilling in. Just as I watched the new shift filter in, someone appeared at my side.

"So, ye think ye are a ticket, dae ye?"

Without looking, I pulled the metal baton from my pocket and swung it as hard as I could to my right side. As I spun to see the rather large and fat man crumple to the floor, I had already pulled my knife. I slashed it across his eyes and then began to stab him in the chest. Blood squirted everywhere. I knew he wouldn't be getting back up, but I continued to stab him. When I was done, I wiped my knife on the leg of his jeans and slipped it into the back of my jeans. I put the baton back in my pocket, then searched him. This guy had ten of the tokens. He was obviously a bigger asshole than the last, or maybe just a slower drinker.

"He has been here for quite some time. You're lucky you got him before he got you," the bartender said.

"Another pint," I responded.

He slid the pint across the bar. "Cost you a token this time. As much as you are entertaining, you got the chips from the guys you killed, and you've had your freebie.

I slid two tokens across the bar. I thought it best to keep the bar man on side.

"Is this your place or do you just work here?"

"My place," was all I got in response.

I lifted my pint and turned once again to look over the other patrons. A few were still watching me, but most had gone back to whatever they had been doing before. I considered taking a table, but I liked standing with my back to the bar, where no one could come up behind me. I eyed the waitresses. They all looked a bit worn out, but I couldn't remember the last time I had seen a female.

I was almost finished with my second pint when I seen her... my mother. I rubbed my eyes. It couldn't be, but it was. I walked towards her in a haze. She had her back to me. She had a bucket and she was tipping the full ashtrays into it. I just stood and waited until she turned. She dropped the bucket and her hands went to her mouth. I watched her eyes fill with tears

"What are you doing here?" was all I could think to ask.

She grabbed my arm and pulled me to the side.

"They took me during the night. They kidnapped me. You have to go. It's not safe here."

I could hear the fear in her voice. To her, I was still her little boy who had to be protected. I couldn't take my eyes off her. She was alive. I never imagined seeing her again, at least not until I was dead.

"Get yourself somewhere safe," I told her as I felt the rage build in my chest. Someone had put their hands on my mother, and they were here.

"What? No... You have to go. You'll get hurt."

I turned my back on her. Something I had never done before.

I walked towards the bar at a brisk pace. I was still holding my pint glass, so I threw it straight at the bar man. He seen it coming and ducked. I was in the middle of vaulting the bar when he came back up. Both of my feet slammed into his chest and sent him shooting back into the gantry. Bottles smashed all around him as he sunk to the floor. His eyes were wide.

"You can't hurt me. They'll kill you."

I lifted one of the bottles that had fallen on the shelf and brought it down with an incredible force over his head. It smashed on the first go but the neck of the bottle was still in my hand and a large piece of glass was sticking out. I began plunging it into his face. I had no idea a man could scream so loud. I have no idea how many times I stabbed him, but I only stopped when someone put their hand on my shoulder. I spun quick and seen it wasn't my mother so I headered the guy. He flew back into the bar. Before he righted himself, I had pulled my knife from the back of my jeans and slit his throat open. This time, I didn't go wild. I scanned the bar to see who else was coming for me. No one. The rest of the patrons were just standing watching. When they realised it was over, they started to sit down again. I looked over to my mother. Her jaw was hanging open. I wiped my knife clean and slid it into my jeans. There were two guns under the bar. I could see them while I was looking down at the dead man on the floor. I took both and the extra bullets that were there. I jumped the bar and walked straight over to my mother, keeping one of the guns in my hand, in case anyone got any big ideas. I took her by the arm and walked us both right out of the door. No one followed.

Everything that I've told you happened about a month ago. We are on the move again, looking for good people, if there are any left. My mother doesn't look at me the same anymore. I'm not sure I'm her little boy now. I'm not sure I want to be. It's a bad world we live in and I would do anything to protect her. No one will ever lay a hand on her again. She won't talk about what happened to her, and that's probably for the best. Some nights, I lie awake and wonder if I'm still a good guy. I'm really not sure. It doesn't matter. There are a lot of bad guys out there and if any of them come near us, they will get to see my dark side.

Author Bio

Kevin J Kennedy is a horror author & editor from Scotland. He is the co-author of You Only Get One Shot, Screechers and has a solo collection available called Dark Thoughts. He is also the publisher of several bestselling anthology series; Collected Horror Shorts, 100 Word Horrors & The Horror Collection, as well as the stand-alone anthology Carnival of Horror. His stories have been featured in many other notable books in the horror genre.

He lives in a small town in Scotland, with his wife and his two little cats, Carlito and Ariel.

Keep up to date with new releases or contact Kevin through his website: www.kevinjkennedy.co.uk or find his work on Amazon at https://www.amazon.com/-/e/B016V0NA7M

Countdown by Veronica Smith

Countdown: 3 Days until New Year's

Jamie had three different New Year's Eve party invitations; and those were just the formal ones that were received through Facebook Events. She'd had two other 'drop on by' verbal invitations as well. She discussed the choices with her boyfriend, Marcus, to see which one he wanted to go to and the only answer she got was 'whichever one had the most free beer'.

Since it was up to her, and she didn't want to go 'party hopping', she had to decide which one to attend. She had friends at all of them, and while she knew no one would be hurt if she chose another, she still couldn't decide. She spent an entire day figuring out which one to attend. Two of them were within the city limits of Houston, so shooting fireworks off in the street was out of the question. That knocked out two choices, leaving only three more to decide from. One of them was east of Houston, in Baytown, pretty damn far away. She lived in Katy which was west of Houston. That would be a dangerous drive coming home; at least fifty miles of possible drunk drivers on the freeway. She mentally crossed that one off the list. The last two choices were both on the west side; both further north from her but neither would require a drive through Houston to get to them.

Jamie grew up in Houston. Her parents still lived in Meyerland in the same house she grew up in. But she'd had enough of the clogged freeways and other big city troubles. As soon as she was old enough, she moved out to Katy and never regretted it.

Hmm. Darrell's party or Robbie's party? She weighed them on both hands. She liked everyone going to both and they would both be overflowing with alcohol. She almost chose the closer one, Darrell's, just so she could drink a little longer, when a post popped up in Robbie's Event page on Facebook. Robbie was offering to let any and all drinking spend the night; just bring a sleeping bag. She knew Marcus would want to drink since he rarely got a chance to. He was a police officer and took his job seriously. He would really only drink at a party if he had the next day off. She was afraid she'd have to lighten up on the drinking herself and drive them, but now she didn't have to. She clicked 'Join' on the Event and finally made her decision.

Countdown: 2 Days until New Year's

After deciding to make a huge pot of queso for the party, Jamie got her grocery list together and went to the store. Marcus was working so she shopped alone. She was halfway through her list when her cell phone rang.

"Jamie, please tell me you are carrying your gun," Marcus asked, before even saying hello.

"It's in the car. Why?" she replied, "I don't carry it in the store. What's going on?"

"I heard on the radio that there are riots going on all over the country. These crazy laws our new president somehow got passed have pissed off a lot of people. People are rioting and violence is breaking out all over the place. Most of the stores in Houston's inner city have shut down until it's under control."

"There's nothing like that going on here," Jamie remarked as she noticed the calm shoppers around her, "By the way, we're having spaghetti for dinner tonight."

"Sounds great," Marcus replied, "Don't forget the parmesan. But please start carrying your gun everywhere. I'd feel better if you did."

"You'd hate for all those hours in the gun range to go to waste, huh?" Jamie teased him while she scribbled 'parmesan' on her grocery list.

She wouldn't admit to him that she had forgotten to add it.

"Ha ha," he mock-laughed, "But seriously, I do want you to carry it."

"Okay, I promise," she laughed back, "Now let me finish my shopping."

"Got it babe," he said, sending a noisy smooch through the phone, "Love you."

"Love you too," Jamie smiled as she hung up.

She finished the shopping and, as she had promised, put the gun in her purse before she begun bringing the groceries into the house. She didn't buy very much so it only took two trips to get it all inside. On the second trip she paused when she heard distant gunfire. Since it was only two days before New Year's it could just as well have been fireworks but she was pretty sure that it was gunshots instead. It could have been hunters too;

there were a lot of bird hunting companies out here. It sounded quite a distance away, even with the garage door shut, so she wasn't too worried about herself, but it made her think of what Marcus had said. She shook her head, wondering what was going on with this country. She locked up her car and went in to make Marcus' favorite dinner of spaghetti with spinach salad.

"That was delicious!" Marcus said, pushing back from his second plate of spaghetti.

Jamie had no idea where he put it all. He was six foot two and in incredible shape. They both went to the gym once or twice a week, lately closer to once a week. He still ate like he was starving and never gained a pound. If she ate like that, she'd be a blimp. As she was putting the leftovers away in the refrigerator and setting the dishes in the sink to soak, Marcus put on the news. When Jamie came in to sit next to him on the sofa she was shocked at the images on the screen.

"Is that in Houston?" she asked him.

"No, this is London," he replied, "It's not just here now. It's like the violence is spreading all over the world."

"London Bridge is falling down," she sang sarcastically.

"If they don't stop, that damn bridge *will* be coming down," Marcus pointed at the screen, "See all those people fighting there? They're all blocking the bridge entrance."

"But why would they want to do that?" Jamie asked.

Marcus shrugged, "Who knows. Why would people here riot at a mall? When they get violent I think they get brain damaged."

During the next commercial Marcus got up, pulling Jamie by her hand to follow him. Since he was pulling her into the bedroom she immediately thought it was her lucky night.

Instead he started bringing out all of their many guns to the bed along with appropriate boxes of ammo.

"What are you doing?" Jamie asked warily.

Once he had everything out, he started separating it.

"What are you doing?" Jamie repeated.

"I don't want to have all of our guns in one place. I want to spread them out so if anything happens we'll have what we need no matter where we are. Now help me decide what to put where."

In the end, they decided that three pistols each would go in both cars. Since he had three shotguns, Marcus decided to put one in Jamie's trunk and the other two in his. He had four rifles and again split them evenly between both vehicles. He also split up all the ammo for each gun and car. Lately he'd been moaning about how he wanted to buy an SUV and replace his car, but tonight he was happy as he still had a trunk to lock it all up hidden. Both cars were in the garage so they were able to fill up the trunks unseen. He reached up on the shelf to the bug-out bags they kept in case of hurricanes.

"We only have two of them," Jamie said, "Want one in each car?"

Marcus asked, "How quick can we put together two more?"

"Are you serious?" she asked.

"Very serious. I want two bags in each car."

He also reached on the shelves where they kept the extra cases of water. He put one in each trunk.

"Are you sure the ass of my car won't bottom out?" she teased him.

He looked at her and thought for a minute, then put in one more case each.

"Well, if it wouldn't before it will now," he teased back.

157

It only took an hour to put together two more bug-out bags and they managed to squeeze them into both trunks.

"Now about that bedroom . . ." Marcus smiled, as he pulled her by the hand again to the bedroom.

Countdown: 1 Day until New Year's

New Year's Eve was a busy shopping day for most grocery stores. They would all be closed tomorrow so they were crowded with people buying last minute party supplies. Although they were open now, they all planned to close by 6pm so their employees could bring in the New Year in celebration as well.

Jamie and Marcus were patiently waiting in the checkout line with only a few items in it. Even the 'twenty items or less' line was pretty long. Jamie may have added the parmesan to the list the other day but forgot the chips to go with the queso that was melting in the crockpot at home. Marcus groaned and threatened to make her go shop by herself, then smiled and got the car keys. Since they were there for chips anyway they decided to get four more cases of water to replace the ones from the garage. They frequently went fishing or camping and could go through an entire case in one trip.

After paying, they pushed the cart to their car and Marcus almost pushed the button on the remote to pop open the trunk out of habit.

"Uh uh," Jamie shook her head, "Unless you want to show off your collection."

He nodded and unlocked the doors only. They put all the water on the back seat floor boards and put the chips on the backseat. As soon as they got home they started to unload and Jamie suggested they just leave the chips there.

"Why walk them inside then have to walk them back out here?" she asked.

Marcus agreed, thinking what a smart girlfriend he had. After checking to make sure the crockpot was melting the spicy cheese fast enough they both jumped in the shower. The original thought was to save time by showering together but that didn't work as well as originally intended. Once they soaped each other up all bets were off. It was a full hour before they got out; clean but happier. As they dressed for the party, Marcus asked, "What time do we need to be there?"

Jamie was the more organized of the two and would have all the information.

"We need to be there sometime between 7:30 and 8:00. I'd rather get there closer to 7:30 since we have queso and it's usually pretty popular."

They pulled up to Robbie's house around 7:45. There were several cars and trucks already parked off to the side and around the corner to save the area right in front of the house to shoot up the many fireworks that would be brought to the party.

"Oh shit!" Marcus cursed, as he walked through the garage to get to the kitchen and set up the queso.

"I forgot fireworks," he called out, "Is anyone else going to get some? I'll ride with them and buy some."

Jamie shook her head. Usually she was the one who forgot things; that was why she always made lists. Jamie set up the crockpot and helped the rest of the women with the food and last minute heating up and cooking. While Jamie was in the henhouse, Marcus was back out in the garage with the men. He pulled out a beer from the garage fridge and snuck out the cigars some of the women didn't want to see. They took inventory of the fireworks and decided there weren't enough. Four of the men, including Marcus, hopped in the truck with Robbie and they went to the nearest fireworks stand to sweeten their stash.

After getting the food and kitchen the way they wanted the women each got a plate of food before the men could wipe it out, and went outside to sit down with their men.

"Where is everyone?" Robbie's wife, Karen, asked, "And why does it smell like cigars out here?"

The remaining men looked around guiltily as they tried to put out the evidence without being seen.

"They went to the fireworks stand near the stoplight to buy some more," Craig replied.

"Marcus and I completely forgot to buy any so I know he wanted to go and get some," Jamie mentioned.

They shrugged and sat down to get comfortable with their plates and drinks. By the time the guys got back the women were all feeling the effects of the chocolate pudding shots they had eaten. Some more guests had showed up as well and the party was well under way.

Since this was Texas, few paid any attention to the New York City ball dropping. For most Texans, it wasn't New Years until it was 'their' midnight. The TV was on in the house but only a few were watching it. At midnight on the east coast, as the ball was dropping, the picture suddenly blinked out. One of the women watching tried other channels but couldn't get anything on any channel at all. She shrugged and pulled out her phone. She noticed she had no signal. That didn't surprise her. Robbie and Karen's house was pretty far out in the sticks and frequently lost signal. The TV was quickly forgotten and after a while, everyone was outside partying. At midnight they shot off as many fireworks as they could at the same time. The men lined up down the street, timing it so they could shoot off together. It was glorious and everyone oohed and aahed.

Marcus kissed Jamie sweetly as they said "Happy New Year!" to each other.

Countdown: New Year's Day

Around 6am some of the guests began stirring. Some were in sleeping bags while others were on the sofa, loveseat, and chairs. Still others were in the extra bedrooms and a couple more were draped on a bed with Robbie and Karen. There was so much drinking the night before and well into the morning that no one went home.

Jamie sat up, her head pounding, and she tiptoed around sleeping guests to the bathroom; she badly needed to go. When she came out she realized the sound of the toilet flushing woke those closest to the hall and that started the mass awakening.

"Can't get anything on the TV," Charlie muttered, pushing buttons on the remote.

"The power is out dummy!" his girlfriend, Monica, chided, pointing to all the dark lamps and lights.

At least half of the waking guests pulled out their cell phones only to realize that they had no signal.

"You know Robbie's signal goes out all the time," Marcus reminded, having finally woken himself.

After everyone was awake, they decided to go clean the street of firework debris; hangovers be damned.

"My head hurts so frigging bad!" Craig moaned, holding his head with one hand while he held open a garbage bag for Marcus to dump in some debris.

The street was a mess. Besides the pieces of explosives littering the ground there were scorch marks everywhere as well.

"What's that noise?" Karen asked, looking up.

"I don't hear anything," Craig said, "Wait, now I do!"

Everyone stopped and looked up to see rows upon rows of jets crossing the sky from the west. There were so many that it was at least five minutes before they saw the last of them fly past their view. Almost immediately after, they heard distant explosions, far louder than any fireworks.

"What was that?" Jamie exclaimed as others screamed.

Marcus ran to his car and got out his police radio. With the cell phones and power out the radio was their only hope of getting any information. They all listened intently and were in shock to find out that throughout the night most of the country was being bombed. They seemed to be working north to south and west to east. If they hadn't all been passed out or drunk they might have heard the many sirens going off in the city. They learned that the power outage was due to a statewide blackout. The explosions kept coming, but were far enough away that they were in no danger; at least for now.

"We need to go somewhere high up," Marcus said, "Somewhere where we can get a view of the city."

"The overpass on Highway 99 is pretty high up," Robbie suggested.

"Marcus and I will go while everyone here either secures the house or goes home to secure your own house. Do not drive into the city until we know what we are dealing with."

There were nods and tears as everyone decided what to do. Marcus went up to Jamie and asked her quietly, "Remember what's in our trunk?"

She nodded, tears forming in her eyes. "Bring all that in the house. We don't need to worry about going home yet. I think that more people together will be safer."

"But my parents . . ." she whispered, "They live in Houston."

"I'll see what I can see. Then we'll decide if it's safe enough to go and get them. Okay?"

She nodded again as he handed her the car keys, "Get it all inside and get with Karen to hide the guns until we're sure who can shoot and who can't."

Marcus and Robbie jumped into the truck and drove off towards the highway. Jamie got with Karen, and with the help of three other trusted friends they backed the car up in the driveway close to the house and snuck the guns and ammo into Karen and Robbie's bedroom.

"I laughed at him for putting all this water in the trunk but now I'm glad he did," Jamie laughed as they looked at the bug-out bags and two cases of water.

"There are four more cases in the back seat that we forgot to put in the house after shopping yesterday."

"Good thing," Karen said, "Everyone may have been drinking booze last night but they still went through most of our water. We'll have to ration this. Let's get this in the house and then start filling up all my empty plastic jugs from the taps. We'll save the bottled water for drinking only."

When they reached the top of the highest overpass on Highway 99, Marcus and Robbie sat stunned. The entire horizon was in flames. Destroyed buildings could be seen even from here. They sat in silence, unsure of what to say. Suddenly the radio came to life.

"Help! Please someone help!"

"We're here!" Marcus yelled back, "Where are you?"

"We're in what's left of the Galleria hotel. We were in the ballroom but the building has come down on us," he coughed before continuing, "It's dark and we can't get out. I was running security for the hotel when it happened. What happened anyway?"

"Invasion," Marcus responded, "I think we are being invaded."

He tossed the radio in the back seat and said to Robbie, "Time to get back to your house and get ready. "

"For what?" Robbie asked, his eyes welling with tears.

"For anything. It's a whole new world now." Marcus replied bleakly, "Happy New Year."

Author Bio

Veronica Smith once fancied herself the next Carolyn Keene when she was but a pre-teen. When she reached adulthood, she wanted to be the next Stephen King or Anne Rice. Now that she's older and wiser, she realizes it's better to want to be herself, and morphed into The Mistress of Horror.

Besides writing, she developed an obsession for all things horror, and even started many petitions to make Halloween a year-long holiday. Despite the support of several Senators and a retired US President, the bill was vetoed in the House. To her chagrin, Halloween still remains a one-day holiday only. But she decided to improvise, putting out her Halloween decorations in the yard at Christmastime as well. So far no one has had her arrested for it.

She and her husband live in Katy, Texas with their son and several pets, including a small horse-sized mastiff.

Follow her at:
viewAuthor.at/VeronicaSmith
www.amazon.co.uk/-/e/B014JCZQT4
www.facebook.com/Veronica.Smith.Author
twitter.com/Vee_L_Smith

Forsaken Gravitas by Robert W. Easton

Jack had had too much to drink, and he knew it. Trouble was, he didn't rightly care. Sometimes you just needed to fight your way to the bottom of the bottle. This night, he realized that he had made a mistake.

"Great," said the Indios. "I'll be at the airfield tomorrow afternoon."

Inwardly, Jack slammed his head into the table. Outwardly, he slid the pack of cigarettes farther from him, as if that would help. Symbolic really, but that mattered. It was a choice, and he was making it. He had done this before, and that's why he didn't chuck them into the trash. Imported cigarettes were expensive in the Amazon.

"Right, dress warm," he slurred. The native Brazilian waved and walked out, pulling his iPhone from his back pocket and checking it as he pushed the screen door open. It banged closed with a rattle.

Jack eyed the small bar. There were two video lottery terminals, a pool table with a horrific rip on the felt, and the cannibalized remnants of a vintage jukebox. Behind the bar, the

166

next song on the playlist on the satellite radio played through a Chinese LED TV. "It's the end of the world as we know it, and I feel fine." Worst. R.E.M. song. Ever. Even this inappropriately upbeat Canadian sea chanty version.

Disgusted, he stood up. Fighting the random wobblings of gravity, he stumbled his way to the back door.

"Night, Jack," yelled Tio, the Peruvian bartender-owner.

Jack gestured vaguely back at the door, and tripped his way to his trailer. He managed to get the door open as the black abyss circled around him. As he fell onto the pullout, it dove down and took him.

Jack woke with a start, falling off of the pullout. A boot crashed onto his head. The irritating, squeaky calls of a pair of mated sun conures ricocheted through his aluminum trailer. He reached over and banged on the wall. For three or four brief seconds, the birds stopped. He slumped down on the floor, basking in the temporary reprieve. His trailer was totalled on the inside, he decided. The ceiling was damaged from the inside, dozens of small concave indentations, as if... he nodded, understanding. Some prior resident probably banging with a broom.

Every morning.

He stomped out of the trailer with one boot, kicking it off, and lurched into the outdoor shower. A shock of cool water froze the breath in his throat. Paralyzed, he succumbed to the moment, wishing for death to finally free him.

But his lungs didn't listen, and breath came again. Jack leaned against the shower wall, and wept for a lost love that chased him even into the heart of the wild Amazon.

That afternoon, as he prepped his Beechcraft King Air Model 65-90-2, the Indios drove up to his hangar on a Kawasaki dirt bike. He killed the engine and let it coast to a stop at the side of the runway. He slid off and lowered to bike to rest on the ground. Jack narrowed his eyes at the casual disrespect of the machine.

The swarthy Incan (Jack remembered the man saying that he was an Incan shaman) shrugged, and said, "Kickstand broke."

A low rumble accompanied the onset of vertigo. Jack first thought it was the schnapps, and that meant he shouldn't fly today.

But the Indios (*What was his name?*) had his arms splayed to each side, dancing for balance. They locked gazes for a moment, and Xavier (*That's right*) nodded, oddly, as if acknowledging that he had just been proven right about something. (*What had we been talking about last night?*)

The disturbance passed, and Jack looked about. Nothing seemed off, except the Beechcraft's wingtips were wobbling.

"See? Earthquake," Xavier bragged. Jack gritted his teeth, irritated by the shaman's confidence.

He focussed on his tablet, wondering if he should restart the preflight check. "Let me finish this, then I'll get you settled in the copilot seat," he called. He bent over the front wheel, looking for signs of wear.

A pair of birkenstocks shuffled into view on the other side of the turboprop. Xavier was peering into the back, and Jack knew what he must be thinking. A gravity gradiometer was a seemingly magical device, allowing him to map the Earth to a depth of almost a kilometer. This device in particular was highly curious. With multiple detectors coupled with a high speed powerhouse computer, it mapped in real time, assigning probable formations to the data. As he flew grid patterns over the Amazon rain forest, he could see the device revealing gold and copper formations, coal beds, oil deposits, uranium ore, and high probability diamond lodes. Precious metals, rare earth elements, transuranics, all would become less valuable with this level of analysis. Rarity was relative, and increasingly less relevant.

Unfortunately for his passenger, Xavier would only see a nondescript aluminum box. That was camouflage, hiding the incredible sensor package within. It was really a shining, black composite case, with a half dozen flashing, status lights. The true case wouldn't reveal anything, either, but it at least looked the part of a high tech computer.

Later on, with Xavier strapped into the copilot seat, Jack eased the throttle forward and sent the King Air rolling down the runway. As the powerful engines reached full power, Jack felt his stomach turn. Strange, he normally loved this moment, as he crossed over the point of no return, fully committed, do or die, to powered flight. It was probably the liquor.

The Beechcraft lifted off the ground, and Xavier gave a little fist pump. Jack gritted away the beginnings of a smile, and focussed on gauges, willing his nerves to settle. As they gained altitude, he banked slightly to the right. His eyes looked toward the northern horizon, and imagined somewhere beyond was the woman he had left behind. Catherine had not understood his need to accept this project, to put distance between them for awhile. They had fought, said things that could not be unsaid. Now, he was here, and she was gone. He had been despondent ever since.

"So tell me about your prophecy again."

Xavier nodded and tapped his fingernails on armrest. "Right. So thousands of years ago, before the Europeans came and brought us so many gifts, there was a terrible enemy. It passed through our world and left great devastation behind. The earth shook, the tides rose and the rivers receded. The people were decimated, they grew sick and many died. Those that remained told the story, and all the signs that preceded it. My ancestors believed that the enemy would return, and pass the stories from each generation to the next."

Xavier looked out over the Amazon, and into the past. Jack started up the gravity gradiometer, the LED display on the dashboard flickering from flight controls to a splash screen, "Gravitas Corporation". The software spun up, and ran through a series of diagnostics. One by one, the progress bars completed. The onboard GPS revealed the crafts exact position, and a map of Earth appeared, zooming onto South America, then Brazil, and finally their immediate area. The Beechcraft appeared as a blue arrow. The database of previous readings filled in the area, not with rivers and trees, but with gradients of gravity.

As they passed over the rolling Amazon verge, Jack set it to begin recording. He wasn't on target yet, but the extra data wouldn't harm anything.

Xavier looked backwards at the aluminum box. "Is it on?" he called over the headset, loud enough to be heard over the engine noise.

Jack nodded as he flipped the navigation console to display the incoming data. A series of straight lines flickered across the screen. The lines snapped into place, and he could see a gradient of the ground below, like a colour-marked topographic map. He pointed at a dark section. "I've flown this approximate route dozens of times, each time along slightly varying paths.

The gradiometer keeps adding the new data to what it has already detected, creating a greater three-dimensional map of the density of the ground below."

Xavier pointed at the dark splotch. "What's that, then, gold? And how much stronger is the force of gravity above that?"

Jack pulled on his mirrored sunglasses and flipped the navigation console to a GPS readout. He wrote a few numbers on a pad of paper strapped to his thigh, then flipped it back. "Yeah, dunno. Probably metal rich, for sure. You wouldn't be able to tell the difference, gravity wise, if you were sitting above it. Now, if you had a fully functioning high school physics lab plopped there, even then, the difference would be smaller than the error bars on your experiment." He looked over at the native South American. "Sorry, I get technical sometimes."

Xavier flashed his teeth. "I studied Astrophysics at Caltech."

"That's playing against type, isn't it? What did your parents think about that?"

"I'm the tribe's shaman, I told them I needed to learn that stuff for the tribe."

"Your kind of shaman sounds as self-interested as Christian shamans."

The Indios leaned sideways and looked out over the wind, then up into the sky, shielding his eyes. "I think I was justified." He looked at his watch. "Twenty minutes to go."

Jack flipped to GPS again, then looked at Xavier. "Huh?"

Xavier simply pointed up. "Dark matter," he yelled.

The King Air shook slightly as they hit a pocket of pressure. "Dark what?"

Xavier pointed his thumb at the device. "Dark matter. Hey, doesn't turbulence disrupt the readings?"

Jack shrugged. "It has on-board ring laser gyros, amazingly

precise. It knows and corrects for turbulence of much higher frequencies that you can even feel, much less the easy, rough stuff."

"Aren't you going to ask about the dark matter?"

Jack looked at his passenger. "I don't believe in dark matter. It's too lazy. Like creating a magical solution because people don't know everything yet."

Xavier chuckled. "I've said the same thing over many a bong load. There are many theories about dark matter. At its core, though, they start with the observation that there is too much gravity pulling on the stars we see in relation to the matter we can detect. So maybe there is matter we don't see, or can't. Like WIMPs, you know, weakly interacting massive particles, or some other strange configuration of matter we haven't seen in a collider yet. But there is another theory. MACHOs, or massive compact halo objects. In particular, I like brown dwarfs."

"Well, who wouldn't? So brown dwarfs. Oh, like stars, like red dwarfs?"

"Sort of. Sometimes stars when they're forming don't get big enough to ignite. They get really big, but not quite star big. Red dwarfs are stars at the end of their lives, running out of fuel. They are really common, but we can't see them without tools, they're so dim."

Jack didn't answer, focussing on his task. As he grew close to the grid, he had to fly fairly precisely, or risk having to make extra passes. This is why he got the big hey-go-live-in-a-trailer-in-the-armpit-of-the-Amazon bucks. Really the upgraded autopilot did most of the work, but he wasn't going to tell payroll that.

When he looked, he saw his passenger alternating from looking at his Garmin GPS watch to peering at the sky. Xavier hunched his shoulders, and wore deep creases on his young brow. His lip bled from being chewed upon.

"You okay, Xavier? The plane's safe."

The Indios shaman coughed lightly. "Yeah, *we're* safe, way up *here.*"

Jack flipped the screen to the GPS again, nearing the end of a leg. Something caught his eye, and he toggled the gravimetric gradient display back on. "What the fuck!?" he yelled. The screen was swimming in white noise, the new data eating away at the carefully constructed gravity map. "The ground is fucking gone!"

Xavier looked at the ground out his window, then at the display. "No, it's still there."

"Damnit, the gradiometer is shot. Look at this, it's reading like we're flying over a giant hole."

"No, the gravity is normal, it's just there is a new, opposing force." Xavier pointed upwards. Jack felt the bottom drop out of his stomach, and a moment of claustrophobia.

Jack switched to the GPS once more, and deactivated the autopilot. He swung the King Air into a long arc to pick up another scheduled pass over the grid area back to the east.

The interference continued for fifteen more minutes, the center of it travelling across the screen from west to east before fading into background noise. They continued the pattern for some time, Xavier using his phone to check for news when they flew within range of cellular towers.

"Volcanoes are erupting in Japan. Two of them. Minor tremors in California, worries about the San Andreas. Problems with the GPS satellite system, and everyone in America on Twitter is blaming Comcast for some reason."

Jack clenched his jaw, uncertain of what Xavier was telling

him, or if it was even true. There were still a few score uncontacted tribes of Indios in Brazil, and he had no inclination of how these people acted. Xavier seemed more like a college student than some stone age tribesman. He checked the GPS and saw that it was flying on inertial navigation only; GPS wasn't correcting for any measurement drift.

He looked out the window down at the rainforest below. It had a vague blurriness, as if the plane was shuddering. He checked the instrumentation, looking for signs of a failure or a warning indicator. But he could feel through the seat that the Beechcraft was performing flawlessly. "What the hell?"

Xavier looked out and moaned. "It's begun! My people."

Jack glanced over and pulled back on the stick and eased the throttle forward, gaining altitude. "Whatever is going on down there, I want more separation."

Xavier nodded grimly. "The Enemy has returned. It passed us by."

"You think that was a brown dwarf star, zipping by and, what?"

"You know the moon causes tides, right? This was way bigger, and passed nearly as close. I think, anyway. We don't have many object collision detection satellites pointed that way, it was hard to find any data at all, much less enough to work out accurate details."

"What way?"

"Up, away from the ecliptic plane that all of the planets are on. The planets and even the stars in the MIlky Way, all orbit the same way, like this," he said, making a horizontal swirl with his hand. "The Enemy moves like this," he continued, moving his other hand in a vertical swirl."

Jack shrugged dismissively.

"Yeah, there's holes in the theory, but we don't have much data. I barely saw it coming and I knew when to look for it."

"From verbal stories? No way."

"There were other signs. It doesn't matter. If I survive, I'll publish a book."

Jack pointed at the horizon. It was obscured in haze. Xavier peered, as well. "There are both dormant and active volcanoes in the Andes. They could be setting off."

They flew long and hard, back for the airstrip. While they were protected in the air from tremors on the ground, if volcanic ash came their way, their turboprop would quickly become a glider.

Jack tensed his muscles, willing himself to keep it together. If he was on his own, he would have cared about survival less, but he was responsible for Xavier. A pilot was responsible for his crew and passengers. He must give them every chance to survive, and that thought steeled his nerves, allowed to accept his feelings of loss for Catherine.

Looking backwards out the window, Xavier watched volcanic ash rain down on his home. He picked out a spot in the haze, imagining the green infinity beyond and the hidden home of his tribe. He had come home just in time to say goodbye. His people had understood, chosen to stay and take their chances. He had had to leave, to try and save their story. Someone had to keep the stories alive of the forgotten apocalypse. Maybe next time, something could be done. The growing clouds and the frightening speed of the destruction told him that this time, there would be no refuge within the rainforest.

As of now, he was the last of his people.

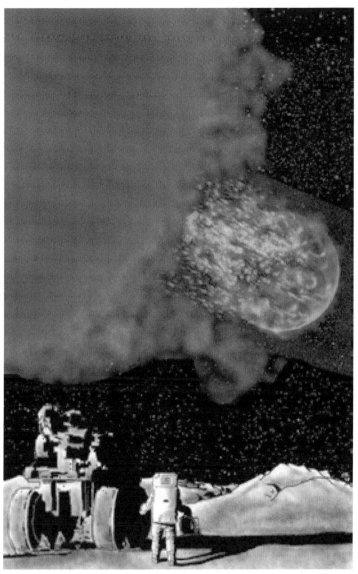

Forsaken Gravitas by Carl Bolton @guerrillaillustrator on
Instagram

Author Bio

Robert W. Easton is long time writer of short stories, poetry and roleplaying adventures for his friends and family. Rob is currently living in the environ of Calgary, Alberta, Canada, with his wife, daughter, and a varying number of black cats.

Rob has been previously published in Strangely Funny III, the online poetry anthology VAMPoetry, Enigma Front: The Monster Within, The 30 Day Collective Vol. 1: The End, Strange Behaviours: An Anthology of Absolute Luridity, Anthology Askew 005: Fantastically Askew, 100 Word Horrors: An Anthology of Horror Drabbles, Hyper-tomb: Crypt of the Cyber-Mummy, and 100 Word Horrors Part 2: An Anthology of Horror Drabbles. In 2018, Rob published his first novel Fortress of the Heart.

Find his books on amazon at amazon.com/author/robertweaston

Flare-Up by Austin James

There's blood in the spider ivy by the bay window when Dale gets home. Blood splotches on the jamb, blots on the carpet. Boisterous blood drowning out the mechanical drone of television from another room.

"Charlie?!"

"Dad?" an adolescent voice calls from the bathroom.

Dale drops his hardhat and lunchbox, hurrying to the bathroom. His son's sitting on the edge of the tub, naked, back to his father, ankle deep in lukewarm bathwater. It smells like raw porkchops turning seasick green. "Charlie? What's wrong?"

"The armpit rash," Charlie says, speaking towards the pale tiled shower wall.

"From that new deodorant?"

Charlie twists towards his father, his torso warped with blood and abscesses. A deep hole stretches from chest to shoulder, exposing muscle and sinew.

"Oh my God, son!"

"It started burning so I tried to open a window to air it out, but it's getting worse."

Dale flips on the shower. "Rinse it off, we've got to get you to the hospital!" He reaches for his phone, but it's not in his pocket. Fuck. The lunchbox, it's still in the lunchbox. "I'm calling an ambulance." He scrambles to his lunchbox, fumbling with the piece-of-shit latch that hasn't worked right since he dropped a hammer on it a few years back.

Come on, open! You fucking thing.

He crushes it open, lunch wrappers spilling out onto the matted carpet. He snags his cell phone, slams the 9-1-1 emergency call button.

Beep—beep—beep.

Fucking busy signal?!

Charlie screams—a hideous squeal. Dale crashes back into the bathroom, finding his son squatting and whimpering in the tub. The armpit rot's spreading, revealing bare shoulder bone, flesh turning putrid and flaking away, muscles withering and peeling from tendons like carved meat.

"We've got to get you to the ER," Dale says, grabbing a nearby towel. "Come on." He pulls Charlie to his feet, fetid skin shifting when touched like it's a sheet draped over muscles, and helps him pass the barrier of the tub, cold shower ricocheting everywhere, fleshy pulp spattering all over the walls, floor, ceiling—morsels of his little boy dripping from Dale's face.

Portions of ribcage start to show, seeping pus and muscle mucous. Chunks of Charlie flopping into the water below.

Dale's stomach whips as he covers Charlie in the towel, wrapping tightly to keep his body from crumbling. The rot has already crept up his neck, part of his jawbone now visible. They hustle past the spilt lunchbox towards the door, towards the old Chevy work truck, towards help—Charlie slowing with each step.

179

"Dad?" Charlie's voice sizzles, his breath like vocal cord decay.

"It'll be okay son, you'll be okay!"

Slices of Charlie's scalp shed from his skull, bloody crumbs of cartilage from his nose and ears stick to the towel. His legs stop responding as the rot rips towards his feet. Dale drags his son towards the door. "Come on, Charlie. Stay with me!" Charlie doesn't respond. Teeth tumble from his mouth, flesh drizzles off his fingers.

Dale's dragging a corpse by the time they get to the entryway.

"Charlie?" he yelps, eyes gushing with grief. He coils into a fetal crouch near Charlie's body as the world twists and compresses, strangling the breath from his lungs. Bile and stomach acid surge up his throat, rupturing from his mouth.

Dale pleads to his God.

Wrapped in tears, blood, and vomit.

Until the tingling on his palms start to burn. Carnage and boils consume his hands, skin-rot sinkholes slashing through intrinsic muscles and tendons. He sways to his feet, towards his Chevy, towards the hospital—ignorant to the newscaster's warning from the TV in another room.

...pheromone-induced chemical reaction to a new deodorant product...flesh-eating fungus...highly contagious...hospitals overwhelmed...stay inside...keep away from others

Author Bio

Austin James writes obscure and uncomfortable fiction. He has caffeine in his blood, gypsy spit in his spinal fluid, and uses an incredibly lazy pseudonym. His prose and poetry have been published in multiple magazines, books, and anthologies.

Find his work on Amazon at https://www.amazon.com/-/e/B071WHTKN6

A Letter to the Reader

Dear Reader,

Thank you so much for taking a chance and spending some of your precious time reading this collection of stories. I hope that they were entertaining and thought provoking. I love short stories and novellas. There is an art to telling a complete story in just a few words. THE END in 13 Stories has been a few years in the making, and its publication is a moment of pride to all involved. There were many bumps along the way, but we pushed through to get this collection in your hands.

If you could take the time to follow up on Amazon by rating and reviewing this collection, I would be eternally grateful. Reviews don't need to be long to be meaningful. As an indie author one of the best ways for me to find out what my readers want more of is to read what they have posted on Amazon. Honest reviews help not only the author to know what hits and misses in a text, but also helps future readers decide if a book would be enjoyable for them as well.

Thank you again & Carpe Noctem,
Valerie Lioudis

Made in the USA
San Bernardino, CA
19 November 2019